FARAWAY LOVE

When Diana learns that the father she never knew has recently died in Australia, she goes out there. At the sheep-station she is made very unwelcome by Lance, her step-brother, and by almost everyone else except Johnnie, who falls wildly in love with her. But Diana finds herself falling for Lance, and when Lisa, a beautiful girlfriend of his, comes to stay, Diana has to cope with her own jealousy as well as Johnnie's jealous actions.

Books by Rhoda Leigh
in the Linford Romance Library:

AUTUMN LOVE

RHODA LEIGH

◆

FARAWAY LOVE

Complete and Unabridged

LINFORD
Leicester

First published in Great Britain in 1983 by
Robert Hale Limited
London

First Linford Edition
published 1999
by arrangement with
Robert Hale Limited
London

British Library CIP Data

Leigh, Rhoda
   Faraway love.—Large print ed.—
Linford romance library
1. Love stories
2. Large type books
I. Title
823.9'14 [F]

ISBN 0–7089–5522–3

Published by
F. A. Thorpe (Publishing) Ltd.
Anstey, Leicestershire

Set by Words & Graphics Ltd.
Anstey, Leicestershire
Printed and bound in Great Britain by
T. J. International Ltd., Padstow, Cornwall

This book is printed on acid-free paper

1

Diana sat staring into space, the accounts in front of her temporarily forgotten. Outside, the trees were covered with the green shimmer of promised spring, and in the park the daffodils were in bud. All day, as she bent over her work at the table she had felt restless, and the accounts on which she was working had suffered accordingly. Now, after the third small mistake in an hour she had pushed them aside and tried in vain to discipline her wandering mind to the job in hand. So far she had been unsuccessful, her thoughts kept sliding into a daydream where she enjoyed a life very different from the one that was hers now.

I suppose it's just spring! She thought, giving herself a mental shake. I guess it makes everyone restless in some way or other. She glanced down at the

1

table. I must have Mr. Hartley's books done to take to him tomorrow, but if I go on making such stupid mistakes —

On impulse she jumped to her feet. She would go for a brisk walk, she decided. Although spring was just around the corner, it was still dark quite early. She would take advantage of the weak sunlight and go out. The books could be finished in the evening by which time perhaps she would have her wandering thoughts under control. She hastily put on a bulky white coat which hid her slim figure, and without bothering with hat or gloves she let herself out of the tiny flat.

As always, she felt a slight sense of freedom as she locked the door behind her. The flat was so small! Many times since her mother's death when she had moved from the spacious house just outside town, into this tiny flat, she had felt, claustrophobically, that its walls were closing in on her. Fancifully she sometimes imagined that she would be forever enclosed in these four walls, and that no one would ever miss her.

As she swung down the road, delighting in movement after sitting still for so long, her thoughts turned from the present to the past. Diana had led a solitary life with her mother until her death, ten months ago. No one ever came to the house except occasional tradesmen, and the twice-a-week cleaning woman.

'We've only got each other,' her mother used to say. 'There's no one else. It's just you and me against the world.' To a child these words had somehow made the world a frightening place, and Diana had always been glad to get home from school to the familiar safety of home. As she grew older her feelings had gradually changed and she longed for friends of her own age; longed to be one of the group of girls who wandered round the shops and had coffee on a Saturday morning, or went by bus to cheer the school hockey team to victory. Her mother, however, had discouraged these activities, she had been barely civil to anyone Diana brought home, and gradually the girl had given up trying, and had just drifted along from day to day between school and home. Her mother, she knew, tried to make their life together attractive. There was a big coloured television; once a week they went to the cinema together, occasionally to the theatre, and quite often on organised expeditions to places of historic interest, or on group visits to London. Whenever her mother exerted herself to arrange these things, Diana felt slightly guilty because she really wanted a different kind of life, and to her mother's half anxious enquiries she replied with an enthusiasm she did not feel. Then her mother had died, suddenly and unexpectedly. She had caught a chill which turned to bronchitis, and then pneumonia, and within two days of being taken to hospital she was dead and Diana was alone.

She remembered her feeling of desolation when she was told of her mother's death. Rightly or wrongly her mother had filled her life. 'We've only got each other.' She seemed to hear the familiar words — and now she had no one. As a child she had asked about her father. 'He died when you were two,' her mother had replied, and her mouth had closed into a thin, hard line, as if she bitterly blamed her husband for dying and leaving her alone with a small child. Once or twice Diana had tried to talk about him, but her mother had killed the subject at birth.

'He's dead,' she would say flatly. 'There's no point in knowing what he was like.' Or sometimes — 'Do you feel that I'm not parent enough for you? Do you need another parent as well?' Since the subject so obviously distressed her mother, Diana had soon learned to avoid it, and for the most part she had been content with life as it was, quickly, and fairly easily, stifling longings for something different.

When she had left school at eighteen, the Careers Advisor had found her a job in an accountants' office. Although shy and nervous to start with, Diana had really loved the work. She had always had an affinity for figures, had always been top of her class in mathematics, and the orderly balance of a page of figures gave her great satisfaction. Her time in the office however was very short. Her mother spoke wistfully of being lonely, and continued to do so even when Linda pointed out that her day in the office was not much longer than her day at school. One day she came home to find her mother in bed and the daily woman who should long since have left, in fluttering attendance.

'Had ever such a nasty turn your ma did.' She answered Diana's enquiries. 'Pains in 'er 'eart. I had a job to 'elp 'er to bed.'

'Have you sent for the doctor?' Diana pulled off her coat before running upstairs.

'No, Miss Diana. She wouldn't 'ave it. Said she'd be all right when you came 'ome.'

Indeed her mother did seem all right.

She steadfastly refused to let Diana summon a doctor, declaring that it must just have been a bad attack of indigestion.

The 'attacks' however were often repeated, and on days when Mrs. Bristow the cleaning woman, was not at the house, Diana found her work suffering as she worried and wondered if her mother was all right alone in the house. She thought of trying to arrange for Mrs. Bristow to come every day, but soon realised that even so, there would be quite lengthy periods between Mrs. Bristow's leaving and her own return from work.

Trying to persuade her mother to see a doctor, she mentioned this, but instead of agreeing to seek medical advice she had another solution. 'If you're worried about me, darling, you don't have to go out to work, you know,' she said. 'We have enough money just to rub along comfortably as we have always done, and surely you could find plenty to do at home?' The dismay which was Diana's instinctive reaction to this suggestion made her at once feel guilty, and gradually, as have so many people ruled by the tyranny of love, she gave in.

Mr. Barton, her superior at the office, could see only too clearly what was happening, and he felt angry and grieved at the loss of the most promising youngster he'd ever had in the office. Holding back the scathing remarks he wanted to make about possessive mothers, he suggested that Diana should continue to do some work for him, but at home. 'I never have to check up on your work,' he pointed out, causing a blush of pleasure momentarily to animate her face. 'Supposing you just take one client for me, and then, if you have time, you could take on more.'

Diana was grateful not to lose altogether the, to her, entrancing world of figures, and she quickly agreed. At first her mother had resented the work that went on at home, but realising perhaps that she might one day drive her daughter too hard, she had finally accepted it, though a rift widened between them every time she made a self-pitying remark about the work.

'There's a good programme on TV this afternoon,' she would say, 'but I suppose you'll be too busy to watch it.' Or — 'Am I going to lose you to those eternal figures today — or can we go to the sales?' Many times Diana was on the point of telling Mr. Barton she could not carry on, but some small core of self-preservation always held her back, and she gritted her teeth, and continued trying to succeed in the impossible task of getting her work done and being available when wanted.

When her mother so suddenly died Diana was infinitely glad that she had clung to her job for the office. It seemed to be the one link she had with the outside world. Several shocks came with her mother's death. The house where she had lived for as long as she could remember, was, she learned, not owned by her mother, but rented. Even most of the furniture did not belong to them. A painful session with her mother's solicitor revealed the fact that for a considerable time they had been living on capital; that there was very little of it left, and would be even less when funeral and a few other debts had been met. 'My client refused to be persuaded into taking out a life insurance,' the solicitor told her, looking at her gravely over the steeple he had made of his fingers, 'so I am afraid all money will be outgoing and none incoming.'

'I'll manage,' Diana had replied, wondering in secret panic what she would do.

'I shall help and advise you all I can, of course,' the elderly man went on. 'For instance, I think it would be best for you to give up the house, and find lodgings or a small flat somewhere — perhaps to share with another girl.' Willingly Diana had given up the house, but she shrank from the thought of lodgings or sharing a flat. She would get a small place of her own first, and learn to be independent.

Later perhaps she would think about sharing. Just now she felt that she would hardly know how to talk to people of her own generation, let alone live with them.

It was while searching for a flat that she had first met Geoff, and she thought of him now as she walked through the park gates and felt her spirits lift at the brave borders of crocuses and the nodding, yellow-tipped daffodils. She had, following the solicitor's advice, put an advertisement for a flat in the local paper, and she had also minutely scanned the advertisements for accommodation, hoping to find something that would suit her. No one had answered her advertisement, and she had found only two vague possibilities, and they were of flats to share. The longer she stayed on alone in the house the more depressed she felt, and at last in desperation she went to the nearest estate agent.

The man who faced her across the desk was about thirty. His thick black hair was cut short and brushed straight back, and his fingernails were immaculately manicured. This much Linda noticed in the first few seconds. He looked at her gravely across the table much as the solicitor had done, and she felt her heart sink.

'I — I suppose it's very difficult?' she faltered, having stated her wants. A sudden smile lit up his face persuading an answering one from her. 'Not so much difficult,' he declared, 'as practically impossible! We have nothing on our books at the moment, but of course, we seldom do have. Flats are relet privately almost before the current tenant leaves. There's a sort of grape-vine of information and always only about half as many flats as are needed.'

'I — I see.' Diana tried not to let her dismay show.

'But don't despair!' The smile flashed again. 'I can't offer you anything right now, but I'll try to tune into the grape-vine and see what I can do. Are you in much of a hurry? Where are you living now and when do you have to leave?'

Suddenly Diana found herself telling him all that had happened in the last year, and he listened with an attentive expression and occasional murmured comments.

'But — but you can't be interested in all this,' she stammered, coming to an end of her recital. It was a long time since she had talked so much. Again his smile enveloped her.

'But of course I'm interested,' he said, 'It's always a help to know a bit about clients . . . '

'Possible clients,' Diana interrupted; but she did not ask how knowledge of a client's affairs could possibly help.

'Prospective clients,' he agreed. 'I shall do my best to ensure that you do become a satisfied client.' He took her name, address and telephone number, and assured her that he would start searching at once. As she stood up to leave, a sudden flurry of hailstones against the window made them both look at the cheerless wintry scene outside; the bare plane trees, the leaden sky, and the falling hail.

'It's a horrible afternoon,' he said. 'I'm just leaving actually. Can I run you home?' Shyly Diana had accepted his offer, and hesitatingly, when they reached the house, she had invited him in for tea. He had accepted with alacrity, and they had sat for an hour getting acquainted.

In a surprisingly short time Geoff had found her the studio flat.

'It's not much,' he had said ruefully as he drove her to see it. 'But it's central and it's cheap. I guess it'll seem very small after what you've been used to.'

'It's exactly what I want,' she had told him gratefully and wholly sincerely. She didn't really know what she did want, but a flat she had to have, and here was one, cheap, and fairly near to the office. She could perhaps ask Mr. Barton for more accounts to deal with. As she looked around the bare room she began silently to plan how she could make it more attractive. Some paint perhaps. She was totally inexperienced, but surely anyone could distemper a wall? Some pictures, a few cushions and a new cover for the divan-bed which acted as a settee in the day time. Her thoughts were interrupted by her companion.

'You'll take it then?'

'What — ? Yes — oh, yes; and thank you so much for finding it.'

'Will you come out to dinner with me to celebrate?'

Surprised and shy, Diana had hesitated.

'Oh, please do,' he had urged. 'I am pleased too to have found somewhere for you so quickly. Do let's celebrate.'

So she had agreed, and that had been the first of many evenings spent together. Dear Geoff! She continued to think of him as she walked briskly through the park. He had helped her to move her few personal belongings to the tiny flat, and he, not she, had painted the walls in an attractive pale green

15

which made the room look bigger. He had admired her new divan cover and the cheerful cushion covers she had made, and together they had searched through junk shops and the weekly market to find pictures for the walls.

She quickened her steps. He was coming tonight to take her to supper, and then on to a late cinema show. She must get Mr. Hartley's books up to date before that. Back in the flat she set to work again with renewed concentration, and when she had finished she put the books into her brief-case ready to deliver next morning. She then had a hasty bath and changed ready to go out.

Geoff was prompt as always, and as she opened the door to him he leaned forward and kissed her on the tip of her nose.

'Hallo, gorgeous!' he said. 'How's everything?' With the ever-ready blush which she hated, staining her cheeks she opened the door wider to let him in.

'I'm not gorgeous,' she said, 'but

16

everything's fine.'

'Good.' He walked past her and sat on the bed with the familiarity born of security in his welcome. 'Everything's fine with me, too. I've made two sales today, both big ones! I've bought you a present to celebrate.'

'Oh, Geoff! You're always finding things to celebrate.'

'Since I met you life has seemed full of things worth celebrating!' he retorted, pulling her down beside him and making her blush again. 'Here!' He thrust a slim, gift-wrapped box into her hands and sat back with a smile as she accepted it and turned it over in her hands.

'Open it!' he urged, and she obeyed with slightly trembling fingers. Geoff had given her things before, flowers and chocolates, and once a pretty ceramic bowl of budding hyacinths, but somehow she sensed this was different, more important.

The removal of the gay paper revealed a blue box, seemingly covered

17

with velvet. She paused for a moment before lifting its lid, and Geoff leaned towards her. Inside was a gold chain and a glowing topaz pendant. 'To match your ring,' Geoff said in unison with her gasp of surprise. 'I've always been a bit jealous of that ring. Even though you don't wear it on a significant finger.' Diana glanced down at the gold and topaz ring on her right hand.

'It was my mother's,' she said, 'though I never saw her wear it. She hardly ever wore jewellery, but it was amongst her things. It's the only thing of hers I wear.'

'Well, now please wear the necklace for me,' Geoff urged her. 'Let me put it on for you.'

'But, Geoff — it's such an expensive present! You shouldn't — '

Leaning across he carefully picked up the chain. 'I told you — I got two very good commissions today,' he murmured, as he undid the clasp. 'Don't say I shouldn't, Diana. I want the right to give you all kinds of things.' Deftly he put the chain around her neck, and as she bent so that he could fasten it, she was glad for the moment that her face was hidden. There was no mistaking Geoff's meaning, no ignoring the sincerity in his voice. She liked him very much indeed; he had kept the demon of loneliness from her, they enjoyed the same things, laughed at the same things, and were perfectly content in each other's company. But — she was not ready for what Geoff seemed so obviously to be suggesting! She felt a sudden panic. How blind she had been! And how selfish! She had just accepted the companionship that he provided, without ever thinking where it might lead. She had blindly drifted along, working, and going out only with Geoff. It had all seemed so easy and pleasant, and he could not be blamed if he thought that she, too, expected, as he seemed to do, that they would ulti- mately marry.

The moment passed. The chain was fastened and she moved hastily away

19

from him under the pretext of looking at it in the mirror.

'It's beautiful, Geoff!' she exclaimed. 'Thank you.' Before he could say any more she had reached for her coat and began chattering about the film they were about to see. Geoff answered her, but it was obvious that his mind was on quite a different subject. In a kind of panic Diana was more animated than she had ever been and she skipped from one topic to another hardly listening to her companion's answers.

Perhaps he sensed that she was afraid of being rushed; but in any case, he made no attempt to go in with her when he saw her home. He kissed her as gently and platonically as always, but his arms tightened around her, and he murmured thickly. 'I've got something special to ask you, Diana. You must know what it is. I'll come tomorrow evening.'

Panic enveloped her again.

'I've got to work late tomorrow,

Geoff,' she said. 'Come the day after.'

'It'll seem an age,' he retorted, and although he did not argue, his arms closed tightly around her and this time his kiss was definitely not platonic.

2

Inside the tiny room Diana stood with her back to the door as if to keep everyone out. 'I'm not ready,' she murmured aloud. 'I haven't really begun to live yet. I'm not ready to settle down and marry.' Slowly she prepared for bed, holding the pendant in her hand for a long time before she put it down and with a sigh pulled up the bed-covers and lay awake in the darkness.

She had been unfair to Geoff she realised now. When she had seemed so content to be exclusively in his company he had every right to believe that that was all she wanted. The truth is that I've just been lazy! she scolded herself. I drifted through life with Mother, and now I've drifted along with Geoff. It's time I pulled myself together. I should decide what I want from life — decide what I'm going to do with my life, and then set about doing it. But what *did* she want from life? Something different, but what? She toyed with plans of going away; of getting a job, in a new place — but what then? Except that Geoff wouldn't be there and she would have the problems of finding a job and somewhere to live, how would life be any different? And was it fair to Geoff to run away like that? She had already been unfair to him in drifting as she had done. How could she insult him by running away from him? Perhaps they could continue being friends, she thought forlornly, but knowing instinctively that this could not be so. Perhaps if he gave her more time she would want to marry him and settle down? Surely he would understand — she hadn't been anywhere nor done anything. But where did she want to go? Round and round went her thoughts, but no answers emerged, and she fell at last into an uneasy sleep.

As she sat crumbling a piece of toast

and drinking her coffee next morning, Diana's thoughts were still of Geoff, and of her future. Shortly after her mother's death she had taken on more work from Mr. Barton, and for most of each week she was fully occupied. He had suggested that she should come again to work at the office if she would like to, but as they were both content with the present arrangement, no change had been made. She hoped that whatever work he gave her today would not be urgent. Today she must somehow decide what she was going to say to Geoff; what she wanted from her life and what she was going to do about it. It's time to stop drifting, she told herself sternly, but she could formulate no concrete ideas about what she should do.

On impulse, she crossed to the minute bathroom and surveyed as much of herself as she could in the half mirror there. Brown eyes looked searchingly into their own reflection and then studied the rest of her face. The eyes, fringed with long, thick lashes, beneath winged eyebrows looked almost too big; her nose was small and straight and her mouth curved and looked ready for laughter even in repose. Her skin was clear, cheekbones rather high, and chin firm. The whole face framed by a profusion of dark curls. She pushed her fingers impatiently through them now. Whatever she did her hair still curled in this riotous fashion. It was easy to manage and she never had given it much thought before. Now she suddenly wished that she could change her appearance; try a new hairstyle, sophisticated, and swept back from her face. She pushed her hair back on each side of her face and looked at the new picture. She looked older. With a sigh she dropped her arms. I want a change, she thought, but not just a change in appearance.

Walking from the bathroom she glanced at her watch, and with a start, realised that she would have to hurry to catch the bus into Cambridge to deliver

Mr. Hartley's books and collect her next allotment of work. Hastily leaving the rest of her coffee, she put away her breakfast things, ran a comb through her now even more unruly hair, and put on her coat. Taking her briefcase and handbag she let herself out of the flat and locked the door behind her. Ignoring the lift, she ran down the one staircase and almost collided with the postman at the door. 'Morning, Miss,' he greeted her cheerfully.

'Good morning.' Diana smiled at him. 'Anything for Number Four?' She hardly slackened her pace as she asked. There was very seldom anything for her. An occasional circular, or a card reminding her that her library book was overdue. That was the sum total of her correspondence. 'Number Four Miss? I'll have a look.' Regretfully Diana stopped. Why on earth had she asked such a stupid question? Of course there wouldn't be anything for her, but now she would have to wait until he had looked in vain, and she would probably miss the bus.

'It doesn't — ' she began, when he interrupted her cheerfully.

'Here we are, Miss D. Barnes. Two for you.'

'Thank you.' Surprise in her voice, she took the two letters and hurried off down the street. The bus was just coming into sight as she reached the stop, and she thankfully joined the small queue and clambered aboard. Having settled in her seat she glanced at the envelopes clutched in her hand. Brown envelopes both, typewritten name and address. The usual advertising circulars! She sighed briefly and thrust them into her pocket. She had more to think about today than sales or a new brand of soap! She stared unseeing out of the window as the bus trundled on. Soon it was full of people going to work or early to shop, and there was a buzz of conversation all around her.

Almost everyone got off at the city centre, and Diana walked the short distance through the narrow streets by the Market Square to Mr. Barton's offices. He greeted her warmly as usual, and gave her twice as much work as she had expected.

'Any time you could set up in opposition!' he joked. 'There are already quite a few people who ask for you.' Diana blushed with pleasure. 'In fact,' he went on, 'I want you to consider coming back here to work instead of working at home. With a bit of rearranging we can give you a room of your own, and then you would be available to talk to people about accounts if necessary.'

Diana was silent, and her elderly companion looked at her quizzically.

'Would you be against that, my dear?' he asked. 'You could be very valuable to us, and — forgive me — I'm old enough to be your father and therefore to take the liberty of saying that I think it would be good for you.'

Diana raised surprised eyes to his.

'You shut yourself away at home far too much for a young girl.' Mr. Barton went on. 'I'm sure it would do you good to have a change and to meet more people. Anyway consider it, will you, my dear, and let me know next week when you bring this work back?'

'Yes. Yes, I will, and thank you.' Diana paused. 'I've been thinking about making a change,' she confided, 'but I'm not sure that this is it.'

Smiling, he patted her shoulder.

'Well, I hope for our sake that it is,' he said. 'Do think about it, my dear. It would be a very good position, particularly as you are still so young.' He opened the office door and bade her goodbye. Linda walked out into the grey morning again, thinking of what he had said.

Perhaps this was the answer. Perhaps she should tell Geoff that she wanted to further her career before having any thoughts about settling down? But even that sounded like a half-promise, and in a moment of self-revelatory honesty she realised that however much she liked him she did not want to 'settle down' with Geoff, now — or ever.

Sighing, she stood for a second, irresolute on the pavement, and then shivering slightly she turned into a nearby café. It was still early, but a cup of hot coffee would be good, she'd only drunk half a cup before leaving the flat. She sat at a table in the window and gave her order. 'Coffee and toast, please.' While she waited for it she idly examined her two letters, and in that moment her whole life was changed in a way that she could never have imagined.

The first was advertising a woman's magazine, and she barely glanced at it. The second, to her surprise, revealed a typewritten letter and she had to read it several times before she could assimilate its contents. The heading was impressive; a company of solicitors in Cambridge, Wentworth, Wentworth and Bridges. The message was brief.

'Dear Miss Barnes,' she read,
'*If you would be good enough to make an appointment to see me at*

the above address, at your earliest convenience and bring with you some proof of your identity, you will learn something to your advantage.'

The signature was an almost illegible scrawl, but luckily beneath it was typed a name — *'B. Wentworth'*.

At first Diana thought that it must be a mistake. She looked again at the envelope. It was her name and her correct address, but who besides Mr. Barton and Geoff knew that? Well, obviously Mr. Wentworth, whoever he was, did. Mr. Wentworth — solicitor of the firm of Wentworth, Wentworth and Bridges. She looked again at the heading, and again read the short letter. What on earth could it mean? *'Something to your advantage'* — that sounded like money. Perhaps it had been discovered that her mother had had more assets than Diana knew of? But Wentworth was not her mother's solicitor. For a few seconds more she sat staring at the letter and then for the second time that morning she jumped to her feet leaving her coffee untouched. Hastily she paid her bill and went out into the street. There was a telephone box at the corner, and she waited impatiently outside until its occupant had finished his conversation. Once inside, she fumbled for coins and with trembling fingers dialled the number given on the letter head.

'Good morning. Wentworth, Wentworth and Bridges. Can I help you?'

'I'd like to speak to Mr. B. Wentworth, please.'

'May I have your name?'

'Oh, yes. Diana Barnes.'

'One moment, Miss Barnes. I'll see if Mr. Wentworth is free.' There was a short pause and a series of clicks, and then again the cheerful voice.

'Miss Barnes? Mr. Wentworth can speak to you now. I'll put you through.' A second's wait and then a deeper voice greeted her.

'Good morning, Miss Barnes.'

'Good morning. I — I've just had your letter.'

'Ah — yes. Now how soon could you come to see me, Miss Barnes?'

'As soon as you like. I'm in Cambridge now,' Diana answered.

'Good, good. Let me see now. I'm free in about half an hour. Could you come then? That's at ten forty-five?'

'Yes. That's fine.'

'Do you know where my office is?'

'No — but I'll — '

'It's just behind the Cathedral.' The voice broke in. 'Opposite to a little pastry shop. You'll see the brass plate.'

'Thank you. I'll be there at ten forty-five.'

'Goodbye till then, Miss Barnes.'

There was a click as he hung up the receiver and Diana put hers back slowly. Half an hour. She would walk instead of taking the bus, she decided. That should just fill in the half-hour that she had to wait before finding out what this was all about.

The waiting room into which she was shown was dark and chilly in spite of the small electric stove burning there. The furniture was cumbersome, and there were no magazines to occupy the time of anyone who had to wait. The two other occupants took no notice of her at all, and Diana sat, irrationally feeling more and more nervous. However she did not have to wait long, before she was summoned and led up a narrow staircase to a much more cheerful room.

'Miss Barnes,' her guide announced at the door, and a middle-aged man came round from behind a large desk to greet her.

'Good morning, Miss Barnes.' His handclasp was warm.

'Good morning.'

'It's a chilly one though, isn't it?' he went on. 'Please sit down, Miss Barnes.' Diana sat in the chair he indicated, and Mr. Wentworth went back behind his desk.

'Well now!' He began, clasping his hands on top of it. 'You *are* Miss Diana Barnes?'

'Yes.'

'Your full name is — ?'

'Helen Diana Barnes, but I've always been called Diana.'

The man behind the desk nodded. 'And have you some proof of your identity?' he asked.

'Well,' Diana hesitated. 'At home I have my birth certificate — but in my bag I have my Savings Bank Book.'

'That will do admirably. Do you mind if I see it?'

Diana opened her bag and handed over the small green booklet in its plastic cover. Mr. Wentworth took it and glanced cursorily at the name and address inside before handing it back.

'I expect you're wondering what all this is about,' he smiled.

'I haven't the faintest idea.'

'I have two pieces of news for you. First, that your father died recently and second, that together with his stepson you are joint heir to all his possessions and property.'

Diana felt her mouth drop open in surprise. Closing it firmly she stared at the solicitor intently and tried to sort out which of her chaotic thoughts to utter.

'My — my father died eighteen years ago,' she said at last.

The solicitor shook his head. 'If you are Helen Barnes,' he said, 'and I have no reason to doubt it, your father died six weeks ago in Australia.'

'Australia!' Diana echoed. This interview was getting more unreal every minute.

'Do you remember your father, Miss Barnes?'

'No — no — I was only two years old when he — when he — ' She hesitated, then went on. 'My mother told me that he died when I was two years old,' she finished.

'Would you like a cup of coffee?' Mr. Wentworth said suddenly.

'Yes — yes, please.' Diana was grateful for a few moments in which to try to collect her thoughts. The solicitor rang the bell and ordered coffee and biscuits, and sat silently until they arrived. After the trivia of milk and sugar had been dealt with, he went back to the subject of the interview.

'Let me tell you from my point of view what has happened.' He suggested. Diana looked at him in silence. Taking this for assent, he went on, 'Several weeks ago I received a communication from solicitors in Melbourne, asking me to trace a Miss Helen Diana Barnes, known as Diana Barnes, and last heard of as a small child in Hinton, Cambridgeshire.'

'I've lived there all my life,' Diana said.

'Yes — well, you were therefore not difficult to trace. Anyway, having found you I was to communicate to you the contents of your father's will. Which I shall now proceed to do.'

'But — but I don't understand,' Diana said urgently. 'Are you telling me that all these years my father was alive?'

'That is so.' He nodded gravely. 'It seems,' he went on, 'that eighteen years ago your father left your mother for another woman. Your mother divorced

37

him and he re-married and emigrated to Australia. Evidently — ' he paused as if seeking for words, 'Evidently as he had gone completely from your mother's life, she preferred to think of him as dead.' Into Diana's mind flashed a picture of her mother's hard eyes and tightly compressed lips as she had said, 'Your father's dead'. Conflicting emotions battled for pride of place. She'd had a right to know that her father was alive. She should not have been denied possible contact with him! But he had walked out on her and her mother — left a wife and a two-year-old child to go to another woman! Through the intensity of her thoughts and emotions she became aware of the man's voice.

'I'm sorry,' she apologised. 'I wasn't listening.'

'I expect this has been rather a shock for you,' he sympathised.

'Yes — that is — I don't know what to think.'

'Drink your coffee,' he suggested quickly, and glancing down at her cup,

Diana had to suppress an hysterical giggle at the thought of a third cup of coffee being left. With a slightly shaking hand she raised it to her lips.

'Cigarette?' She shook her head. 'Have a biscuit then. I will, too.' He waited until her cup was drained and the biscuit eaten, and then went on quietly, 'I have here a copy of your father's will which I can read to you, but it has quite a lot of legal jargon in it, so perhaps you would prefer me simply to tell you what it means?'

Diana clasped her hands in her lap. 'Yes, please.'

'Your father re-married and went to Australia, as I have already told you,' he began. 'His second wife was a widow with a ten-year old son, who of course became his stepson — and — your stepbrother, though having no blood relationship to you.'

Diana nodded.

'Your father worked hard and prospered, and at the time of his death was the owner of a sheep station of considerable size. His wife — his second wife — was killed in a car accident four years after they were married.'

'Poor man — he didn't have much luck with his marriages, did he?' Diana's voice was high, and the man opposite looked at her gravely but did not reply to her comment.

'After your father's death — he had a heart attack — and the will was read, Lance Ferguson — your stepbrother and co-inheritor of your father's estate and goods, left it in the hands of the solicitors to find you and appraise you of the contents of the will. Your last known address, of eighteen years ago, was given, and so you were not difficult to trace.'

Diana gazed at him. The full import of what he was saying was hard to understand. Her mind was full of the astonishing fact that her father had died only recently, and not when she was a small child. A feeling of loss that she had never known him, fought with a feeling of anger that he had rejected her and her mother for another woman and her child. She became aware of the solicitor's eyes on her face and realised that he was waiting for her to speak.

'What — what happens now?' she asked weakly.

'Now I shall inform my colleagues in Melbourne of your whereabouts,' he replied, 'and they will get in touch with you, either directly or through me.'

3

Afterwards Diana could remember little of what happened during the rest of that day. She left the solicitor's office in a daze and caught the bus back to her tiny flat. There, she sat in front of the inadequate gas fire staring into space and hearing again the quiet voice telling her that her father had recently died, and realising that even though he had deserted her and her mother, he had remembered her in his will, and had shared all that he had to leave equally between her and her stepbrother. Stepbrother — she lingered over the thought. How she had longed for brothers and sisters when she was a child! She remembered once saying to her mother 'Haven't I even got any cousins?' And her mother's inevitable reply: 'What do you want with cousins? We've got each other.'

She remembered, too, when her class had been told to write a composition entitled 'My Family', she had sat for a moment feeling like some kind of oddity. How could she fill the required number of pages in writing just about her mother? She had looked around the classroom at every bent head and every busy hand, and taking a deep breath, she had begun to write, inventing for herself a family of cousins so clever, so amusing and such fun to be with that she almost believed in them herself. When the marked compositions were returned she had sat in an agony of trepidation feeling that the teacher must know what lies she had written; but she had received a good mark, no comments were made, and she had kept her delightful cousins as dream companions until she was in her teens.

Now she had a stepbrother! She wondered what he was like. Her father must have loved him, to have left him half his estate. She felt a pang of jealousy. Yet — her father had left her an equal share. Did that mean that he loved her, too, even though he had not seen her since she was two years old? Her thoughts centred round the father she could not remember. What had he been like? she wondered. And why had he left them? Perhaps she would never know the answer to that question, but her newly-found stepbrother would be able to tell her about her father. Her thoughts switched to her stepbrother. What was he like? She did a rapid calculation in her head. If he had been ten when she was two, he must now be about twenty-eight. She felt suddenly a fever of impatience to know more about everything. I'd better work, she thought, or I shall just sit here and wonder and make guesses. With an effort she got up and spread her work on the table — but it was a long time before she was ready to concentrate. The solicitor's face kept appearing between her and her books, and she kept hearing his voice say. 'Your father died six weeks ago.'

When at last she was able to con-centrate, she immersed herself totally in her work, not even stopping to eat. She put the light on early as the day grew dull, and was sitting working when a knock at the door startled her.

It was Geoff. He carried a bunch of daffodils and tulips, and looked apologetic.

'Come in.' Diana smiled at him, quite forgetting that she had asked him not to come. At this moment he was just what she wanted. Someone to tell about the extraordinary events of the day.

'I'm sorry. I know you said you'd be working, but I just couldn't stay away.' He thrust the bunch of flowers towards her.

'Oh, thank you, Geoff. I've been working most of the day; I didn't realise how late it is. Come and sit down and I'll make you some coffee. I've had the most exciting news.'

Geoff's eyebrows rose. 'Tell me,' he invited.

'Wait. I'll make the coffee first, and

get out some cake — I'm starving. I just worked on and forgot to eat.' As she bustled about with cups and coffee Geoff thought he had never seen her looking so animated, and his curiosity grew. What on earth could have happened? At last she sat opposite him and plunged into an account of the day's events. At first he interrupted occasionally with questions, but as she finished her story he grew very silent.

'A sheep station of considerable size,' he repeated slowly at last. 'That means you'll be a fairly rich woman, Diana.'

She stared at him. 'I hadn't thought of that,' she said simply and truthfully. 'I've only been thinking about my father and — and my halfbrother.'

'He's not your halfbrother,' Geoff corrected her, much as the solicitor had done. 'You don't have a common parent. He's just the son of the woman your father married.'

'Yes.' Diana flushed. 'Yes, I know,' she said in a low voice. 'I suppose I got too excited at the thought of having some kind of family.' There was a little silence. Geoff broke it.

'He can't mean anything to you,' he said harshly. 'Nor can your father. After all, whether he remembered you in his will or not, the fact remains that he deserted you and your mother. Maybe at the end his conscience bothered him.'

'Oh, Geoff. We can't ever really know what happened. Perhaps it was not all his fault. Mother — mother was not an easy person — she — '

'But she brought you up,' Geoff interrupted. 'Your father ignored you for eighteen years; only now that he's left you some money all his neglect can be forgiven.'

Diana looked at him in dismay.

'Why — why are you so angry?' She faltered. 'It's not like that at all. I have never thought that there was anything to forgive. Until this morning I thought that my father had died when I was just a baby. When I found that he hadn't — '

'You immediately romanticised him and forgot all that your mother did for

47

you, and how *he* abandoned you.'

'My mother denied me the knowledge of my father's existence!' Diana flashed. 'But I certainly haven't forgotten all that she did for me; and as for my father — I just don't know why he left — how can I judge him?'

'Particularly as his death benefits you so greatly!'

'I don't know why you're being so horrible,' Diana cried, jumping to her feet. 'I was pleased that you were here so that I could tell you my news, but now I wish you hadn't come.'

Geoff was on his feet, too, and he caught her hands in his.

'Oh, Diana darling, I'm sorry,' he said. 'I'm being completely selfish. I wanted to ask you — I'd been planning — Oh, Diana, you must know how I feel. I wanted to ask you to marry me; I was thinking only of our life together; but now that you're going to be a rich woman — ' His voice trailed away, and they looked at each other in silence. Diana remembered how she had guessed what Geoff had been going to ask her, and how in a panic she had tried to postpone his inevitable question. She liked him very much, and they had enjoyed many things together but she did not want to marry him, at least, not yet. Since she'd had her whole world shaken by what the solicitor had told her, she had not once thought of what her inheritance would mean to her in terms of money. It had evidently been Geoff's first thought, and he had immediately assumed that it would put a barrier between them. If she had really loved him, she thought, she would have been fighting to prove to him that neither money nor anything else could prove an insurmountable barrier, but now she could think of nothing to say.

Dropping her hands, Geoff was the first to break the silence.

'What will you do?' he asked.

'I — I don't know, Geoff. I hadn't made any plans.' The stricken look in his eyes made her want to throw her arms around him, but she was wise enough to realise that pity is no substitute for love; yet she could not just let him think that she would choose money before him and the life he had wanted to offer her.

'It — it's not just the money, Geoff,' she faltered. 'I'm not ready — I haven't thought about marriage.' She could see however from the look in his eyes, that he did not really believe her. There was a touch of stubborn pride in his voice, too, as he said. 'I don't want to marry a rich wife. Now you'll be able to give yourself all the things I could have given you.'

Her voice made no answer, but her heart cried out how wrong he was. If she had loved him he could have given her precious gifts that no fortune — however big — could buy.

For a moment they stood locked in silence and their own thoughts. Then with a determined effort. Geoff said, 'Anyway your good fortune should be celebrated. Let me take you out to dinner.'

Diana felt that she couldn't bear to talk any more about the day's news. They viewed it from such different viewpoints that she felt there would be no point at which they could comfortably discuss it. She would have liked to eat a quiet meal at home, and go early to bed with her thoughts and imaginings, but Geoff was making a tremendous effort and she could not bring herself to rebuff him.

'I'd love to go out to dinner with you,' she said, 'but not to celebrate. Let's go out as good friends, just as we have always done.'

There was a wry twist to his mouth as he answered. 'All right. We'll go out to dinner just as good friends.'

Diana was soon ready, and he handed her into his car at the kerb as he had done so many times before, but in spite of both their efforts the evening was a dismal failure. Sudden silences occurred which they often simultaneously tried to cover with brittle, surface talk. When the meal was over

Geoff did not attempt to persuade her to go on somewhere else for a nightcap, as he usually did to prolong the evening. Instead he drove straight back to her flat.

'I'll see you again,' he said in a low voice as they stood on the pavement. 'Don't put me out of your life altogether.'

'Of course I won't — ' she began, and he clasped her suddenly in his arms and kissed her fiercely and desperately. She felt herself stiffening in his arms, and almost stumbled as he suddenly released her and strode to his car. She stood, the back of her hand to her lips, and watched till the twin red lights disappeared round the corner and then she went slowly in and up to her flat.

To her surprise it was only a week later that she heard again from the solicitor. The first two days had passed in a fever of impatience; then, as she realised how long she would probably have to wait, she had tried to put all thoughts of her father and stepbrother away from her, and to concentrate on her work. Sometimes she would pause in the middle of adding a row of figures and wonder if that interview with the solicitor had really happened, or if she had dreamed it, but when she received the second letter, asking her to call him at her earliest convenience, every word that had been spoken at their first meeting, together with all her thoughts and speculations, rushed back and flooded her mind.

The second interview was almost as surprising as the first.

'I didn't expect to hear from you so soon,' she said as she sat down in front of the big desk.

'Yes — well — my client, or rather the client of my Australian colleagues, seems to be in a hurry,' he told her. Diana's heart raced. So her stepbrother was as impatient and curious as she was! Maybe he had never heard of her until the reading of the will. Maybe — She became aware of the quiet, dry voice saying, 'expensive conversation.'

'I'm sorry.' She blushed. 'I'm afraid I wasn't listening again.'

Patiently he repeated what he had said. 'I sent a telegram to Australia as I had been asked to do when I found you,' he said, 'and two days later your father's stepson telephoned me. I had expected to hear from his solicitors but he elected to telephone his instructions to me direct, so as to make absolutely sure that there was no misunderstanding. It must have been a very expensive conversation.' He paused, and as Diana looked at him expectantly he went on, slowly, as if feeling for the best words, 'Mr. Ferguson told me that he is sending his secretary-accountant to deal with you, and that he will have the house, the station and all the assets valued by two different firms of valuers to determine the amount that should be paid to you; and that also he is quite willing, should you so desire, for an assessment to be made by any other firm, English or Australian, that you choose.' He fell silent and Diana stared at him blankly.

'He's sending his secretary-accountant to deal with me?' she echoed 'What on earth does that mean? Isn't he coming to England himself?' Until now she had not thought of anything but meeting her 'father's stepson', as the solicitor called him. She had never really considered any of the mechanics of what might happen; but to be told that an employee was being sent to 'deal with her' seemed very strongly to indicate that there was no reciprocal pleasure in whatever tenuous relationship they might have. Perhaps Lance Ferguson was disappointed to find that he had to share his inheritance with some hitherto unknown person.

The solicitor cleared his throat. 'I — er — believe that Mr. Ferguson thought that it would be better for there to be some personal link over the transaction,' he said non-committally. 'His — er — secretary arrived yesterday. He telephoned, and will be coming here to meet you.' He paused. 'You will need a solicitor to represent you, my dear. I willingly offer my services, unless you prefer to make other arrangements?'

'No — no. Please — and thank you. I'll be grateful.' Before either of them could say any more a discreet tap at the door preceeded the entrance of a fair-haired young man, muffled in an overcoat.

'Your girl said to come on up,' he announced. 'So here I am. Clinton West — Mr. Ferguson's secretary.'

'Good morning.' The solicitor stood to greet him. 'I am Mr. Wentworth, and this is Miss Diana Barnes.' The two young people were silent for a second looking each other up and down, then Clinton West offered his hand and shook hers firmly.

'Well — well,' he said. 'So you're the boss's daughter, and you — ' he turned to Mr. Wentworth, 'are the one who found her.'

'In the event, she didn't take much finding,' the solicitor remarked drily.

'Will you sit down, so that we can begin to discuss this matter?'

'Well, now — I don't think I will sit. Plenty of time for discussion. Right now I'd like to take Miss Barnes to lunch so that we can become acquainted. Maybe we can fix a time to meet you again tomorrow?'

Both men were looking at Diana and she smiled a little nervously.

'If that's all right with you, Mr. Wentworth,' she said shyly, 'I'd like to lunch with Mr. West.'

'Of course.' Mr. Wentworth looked from one to the other. 'Will you check with my secretary as you go out, and find what time I have free that will suit you both?'

Having done this, Diana and Clinton emerged into the chilly air. 'Let's get a taxi. Where's a good warm place to lunch?' he asked, turning up his coat collar.

'The Phoenix Hotel,' Diana answered. 'We can walk, it's only just round the corner. You must find the climate very different here?'

'I'll say!' he agreed fervently, putting his hand under her elbow as they walked. 'I haven't been really warm since I got here, and I seem to be weighed down with clothes.'

'It'll be warm in the Phoenix,' Diana promised him as they hurried along. 'Is this the first time you've been to England?' she asked, as they settled by the cheerful fire in the lounge bar for a drink before the meal.

'Bless you, no! I *am* English,' he answered, the slight twang in his voice seeming to deny his words. 'My family emigrated to Australia when I was a nipper. They never really settled though. They were always homesick for England. Six years ago they came back here, but I stayed on. I like it there. Australia seems more like home than England to me.'

'Your parents must have been pleased to see you,' she remarked.

His face darkened.

'Mum died nearly three years ago,' he

murmured. 'The old man and I don't get on. Never did. I shan't visit him. I don't even know where he is.'

Diana was silent. There seemed no appropriate reply.

Her companion went on cheerfully to talk about the comparison between English and Australian weather, and life in the two countries.

'It sounds lovely,' Diana sighed. 'Imagine never being cold!'

'Of course you can be cold even in Australia if you know where to go,' Clinton West laughed. 'And there are drawbacks there, too, just as there are here — in fact, everywhere. The big cities are clean and modern and superb, but it can be very lonely in the Outback.'

'The Outback.' That's what the countryside in Australia is called, is it, Mr. West?'

'Clinton. And may I call you Diana?' She nodded. 'It's certainly countryside,' he went on. 'Each station is very far away from any other. There's no popping out to the store or spending an evening in the cinema.'

'But also no traffic and no queues,' Diana put in.

'That's true. But after a while you get to long for just those things. The Boss was pretty good. The men got fairly frequent spells in the city. Mostly they enjoy the life though, or they don't last long.'

'How do they travel?'

'We have a chopper and a plane,' Clinton told her. 'The chopper is used for quick trips into Melbourne. Also if an aerial search is necessary for any reason. The plane is used if more people are going in, and also to get supplies. There's a Range Rover, too. Lance likes to drive in sometimes, but it's a two-day drive and means camping on the way.' He pretended to shudder. 'Not me,' he said. 'I like my comforts, and sleeping out doesn't come into that category.'

Diana sipped her drink silently. How different we are, she thought. Clinton is happy to ignore his father's existence, and I want to learn all I can about mine; he hates the idea of camping, and I'm sure I would find it very exciting.

4

'A penny for your thoughts.' His voice nudged Diana into awareness of the present. She stared into her glass.

'I think it sounds exciting,' she said. 'To sleep out under the stars, and — '

Clinton laughed.

'The stars are certainly something,' he agreed, 'but I'd rather sit on the verandah with a drink in my hand and look at them.' He went on, chatting easily about the changes he found had taken place in England since he had left as a boy, until they began eating.

'The food's good anyway!' he commented. 'You evidently chose the right place for lunch. Food can get a little monotonous on the station, though there's always plenty of it.'

'Tell me about it,' Diana urged.

'The food?'

'No, the station.'

'Well — it's much like any other station, I guess. It's big though, and it's pretty well run. The men have a good life there.'

'Did you work for my father?'

'Sure did; and he was a good man to work for. He built up a really good place, and he should have had longer in it. His death was a shock.' He paused and then went on, 'Although he always did too much. He had to see to everything himself. Lance used to want to take responsibility for this and that, but the old man always kept the reins tight in his own hands. Well — Lance has got them now, and all the responsibility he wants.'

'Tell me about my father,' Diana begged, and Clinton caught the pleading in her eyes.

'You don't remember him, do you?' he stated rather than asked.

'No — I was only two when he — when he left.'

'I didn't know him till after his wife died — his second wife that is, of course. In fact she'd been dead about six years when I first went to the station, so I can't tell you anything about her.'

Diana remained silent. That would probably have been her next question, she realised. How, she wondered, had this other woman had such an attraction that her father had left his family and gone away with her?

'I think maybe if she'd lived the old man would have lived longer.' Clinton said thoughtfully, 'but after she died it seems that he just threw himself body, heart and soul into his work. Oh, of course there are social occasions on the stations, and Chickaroo did its share of entertaining, but he never took much actual part in it. Mrs. Blestow arranged it all — he just put in a short appearance and paid the bills. He never seemed to take any time off nor to have any relaxation.'

'Mrs. Blestow?'

'She's the housekeeper. A real dragon — she rules us all with a rod of iron and a tongue of vitriol — but she's a wonderful cook and a great organiser. She went to the station with your father and mo — and his wife when they first began.' He paused to reach over and refill her wine glass, and Diana was silent, thinking about what he had said.

'And — and Mr. Ferguson — Lance?' she asked at last.

'Lance? Well he's about six years younger than I am. He was just a nipper when I went there first. Later he went to the city to school, and to college. When he came back he wanted to take over, or at least take over a large part. Don't know what college had taught him about running a sheep station.'

Diana paused, her fork half-way to her mouth. Clinton sounded sarcastic, angry even. She could think of no comment, and after a moment her companion went on.

'Well — he's had the place for a couple of months. I suppose time will tell.'

Diana wanted to probe what seemed his obvious disapproval. Instead she asked, 'What about the staff — the men, how do they — er — get on with him?'

'It's early days to tell yet,' Clinton answered. 'As soon as the boss had died everyone started to call him Mr. Ferguson, but he wouldn't have any of it. 'You've all allways called me Lance,' he said, 'No reason to change now.' ' Again there was that faint note of disapproval in his voice.

'And you don't agree?' she challenged.

'It's bloody patronising — giving us all permission,' Clinton said more sharply. 'I would have gone on calling him Lance anyway.'

'Yes, but if the others — ' Diana started.

'Can't understand why they did,' he broke in. 'Most all of them knew him as a boy — why should they change?'

'But things have changed,' she reminded him gently. 'He's the boss now.'

Clinton stared at her. 'Half-boss,' he retorted. 'Half the place belongs to you, doesn't it?'

Diana stared at him. It was true of course, but she had never thought of it like that. I own half a sheep-station in Australia, she said to herself. It sounded very exciting. Much more exciting than thinking that her father had left her some money — however much.

'Of course you'll sell out to him and then he will be the boss, least in name,' Clinton said, 'but he'll have to prove himself before he'll really take the old man's place.'

'If he ever can — ' was implicit in his voice though he did not actually utter the words. Diana was silent, and so deep in her thoughts that Clinton had to speak to her twice before he regained her attention.

'You know I don't think I will,' she murmured slowly, with shining eyes, and taking no notice of his last words.

'Will what?'

'Sell out to him,' Diana said. 'As you say, half the sheep-station is mine. I'll — I'll go out there.' Just uttering the words aloud gave her fresh courage and initiative. 'That's what I'll do,' she repeated. 'I'll go out there! To Australia! To the Station!' Clinton put down his knife and fork and stared at her. Then he burst into laughter. Diana's face flushed and she looked at him defensively. His laughter subsiding, he reached across the table and took her hand.

'What a smashing idea!' he exclaimed. 'Not one of us even considered that possibility! Lord! I'd love to see Lance's face when he realises that he can't just buy you out.' He chuckled again. 'Mind you — he ought to be pleased,' he went on. 'He'd have to sell out a certain amount in order to pay you half the value of everything, and it's a bad time of year to sell.'

'But you don't think he will be pleased?' she asked.

'When at last he's got the power in his own hands, to have to share it with someone? With a green woman at that? You've got to be joking!'

Diana was appalled. 'Oh I couldn't share any responsibility,' she disclaimed quickly. 'As you said, I'm green. I know nothing about a sheep station. I don't even know anything about sheep.'

'What did you think of doing then?'

'Well, I'd like to see where my father lived. I'd like to see Australia, I'd like to see a sheep station. After that we can see — maybe he — maybe Lance will buy me out as you say he wants to, or if it will hurt the station to sell so much, maybe it can produce me a small income.'

'What d'you care about hurting the station?' Clinton demanded.

'My father built it up,' she said evenly. 'I wouldn't want to undo his work.'

'I guess Lance with his new fangled ideas can do that quickly enough,' Clinton retorted. 'If I were you I'd take the money. Your father evidently wanted you to have half — and whether it's money or stock, it's all the same thing.'

'I don't think so,' Diana's voice was suddenly strong. 'Anyhow I've made up my mind. That's what I'm going to do. I'll — I'll be able to talk to people who knew my father as well.'

He looked at her, newly appraising. 'You really mean it? That's what you're going to do? You won't change your mind tomorrow?'

'Tomorrow I'll be enquiring about air fares!' she told him firmly.

'Well, well!' He sat back in his seat. 'Who would have thought it? Lance will as sure as hell bawl me out. He sent me over here, throwing in two weeks' leave, so as to make sure all went smoothly about the transfer of money, and according to your plans, it's all going to hell in a basket!'

Diana surveyed him gravely.

'I don't think his opinion will worry you very much,' she said shrewdly. 'My arrival will be an accomplished fact by the time you get back to be 'bawled out', and anyway I'm sure you're quite capable of taking care of yourself!'

'If only you knew,' he said enigmatically.

'He should have come himself,' Diana said, the solicitor's words, 'sending his secretary-accountant to deal with you,' still rankled.

'Would it have made any difference?' His eye-brows rose, and Diana's all too ready blush flooded her cheeks.

'I don't suppose so,' she admitted.

'He'd have moved heaven and earth to prevent your going.'

'I don't see why; but in any case the question doesn't arise, and I'm going to Australia!' She sat up straight in her chair, fists on the table looking ready to do instant battle.

Clinton laughed again. 'You look really fierce,' he grinned, 'but don't waste all your big guns on me, I'm delighted with the idea!'

'Even at the risk of being 'bawled out', as you call it?'

'Oh, that!' He dismissed the idea airily. 'I guess by then he'll have more things to blame me for than your unexpected arrival.' Diana looked at him curiously, but before she could say any more, he went on. 'Would you like me to see about a flight for you? And send a cable to say when you're arriving?'

'I'd be very grateful for your help with the flight,' Diana accepted gratefully, 'but do we need to send a cable? Can't I just arrive?' Again Clinton's laugh made the occupants of nearby tables look across at him. They must think we're having a wonderful time, Diana thought as she waited for his spontaneous laugh to die away.

'My dear!' He coughed a little as he began to speak. 'You can't 'just arrive' at a sheep station! There's no handy bus to catch, and no taxis to the Outback! Someone will have to drive, or fly, in to meet you.'

Again her cheeks flushed. 'I wasn't thinking,' she admitted.

'You wanted to make a surprise attack?'

'I don't want to make any kind of attack,' Diana retorted angrily. 'I just want to see the place; to see where my

72

father lived and worked before I make any decisions!'

'Good on yer!' He grinned across the table. 'Why shouldn't you? Now let's get down to details. When do you want to go?'

Diana thought swiftly.

'Is there any day it's better to arrive on than any other?'

'Not really. If you have to wait overnight you can stay at a hotel and have a look round the city.' This would have appealed to Diana at any other time, but now she suddenly wanted to go to Chickaroo as soon as she could.

'I'll have to finish off my various jobs and make some arrangements about my flat. Say one day next week.'

'Sure I'll fix it, but it'll be more likely one *night* next week. Planes for that part of the world always seem to leave late at night.'

'I don't mind,' she replied, thinking how exciting it would be to be setting off on this adventure instead of tamely going to bed.

73

'We'd better go in and see the old solicitor boy tomorrow.' Clinton suggested. 'We have an appointment for three o'clock, remember?'

'Yes. All right. I'll work in the morning,' she planned, 'and get as far ahead as I can. I'll go back into the office, too, and tell Mr. Barton that I can't take on any more work.'

'What work do you do?'

'Oh — a bit of secretarial work at home.'

'At least you don't have to face the rush hour traffic any more than we do on the station,' he remarked.

'No.' Diana's monosyllabic reply covered a rush of thoughts. How glad she would be, she realised, to get away from being shut in her small flat all day. To meet new people and see new things. She was, as she knew, basically a very shy and retiring person, but in just making up her mind to go to Australia, she seemed to have taken a great step forward, and she wondered with a little amazement, why she had been so long content with the quiet, dull life.

Clinton wanted to see her back to her flat, but she assured him that it was almost door to door on the bus route. She bade him goodbye, thanked him for lunch and agreed that they would meet again at three o'clock next day.

Before going to the bus stop she went to Mr. Barton's office. He was surprised to see her.

'You can't have finished that work already,' he greeted her, with a smile. 'Problems?'

'No, not with the work. In fact, not at all,' she added hastily as a look of consternation crossed his face. 'It's just — it's just that I'm going away; and I'd like to go as soon as possible, so I came to ask if you could manage without me when I've finished the work I've got at home.'

Mr. Barton pursed his lips. 'How long are you going to be away?'

'I don't know. I'm going to Australia.'

'To Australia?' He couldn't have looked — nor felt — more surprised if she had said she was going to the moon. Diana rushed into explanations and her employer sat back and listened.

Just the idea of going away has changed her, he thought. She'll never be quite the same again, and perhaps that's just as well. She's always seemed too quiet and too self-contained. He smiled at her across the desk.

'Well, I can't say we won't miss you, because we will, very much,' he said. 'In fact it will be quite difficult to share out the work-load, but of course you must go, my dear.'

'I'm sorry,' she faltered. 'I know it's terribly short notice, but I — '

'But you want to go as soon as you can,' he interrupted her, 'and you're quite right. If you were only going to be away for a week we'd manage somehow, but as it's likely to be longer than that, I must take on some temporary help.'

'If you would rather replace me entirely — ' Diana began.

'No, my dear. I don't want to do that.'

'It would be only fair,' she insisted.

'Maybe. But I don't want to replace you unless I have to. Don't worry. It won't be difficult to find someone while you are away. There's so much unemployment.' He paused. 'I suppose you have no idea how long it'll be before you're back?'

'No. I'm sorry, I . . .' her voice trailed away. She had not bought a ticket for going yet, and she certainly didn't want to start thinking about coming back already.

'Perhaps you won't come back at all,' he suggested with a fatherly smile, showing how unlikely he thought that possibility. 'But,' he went on, 'you may be quite a wealthy young woman and not need to earn your living when you return. Had you thought of that?'

'No. No, I hadn't really. I'm afraid I haven't thought or planned very carefully at all,' Diana admitted. 'I only know that I want to go.'

'Yes. Well — I'll tell you what. Can you finish your current assignment?'

'Oh, yes, of course. I wouldn't leave

that,' she assured him.

'Right. You do that, and I'll get someone else for the office here for an indefinite period. You can probably give me a fortnight's notice of your return.'

'Yes. Yes — I will,' Diana smiled, 'and thank you for being so understanding.'

'Send us a post card.'

'Of course.'

'I'll see you when you come in with the work, so I won't say goodbye now.'

Diana felt as if she were walking on air as she went to the city centre bus stop. She remembered nothing of the ride home, and the floating sensation stayed with her for the rest of the day. She could not settle to work, nor to sorting and packing clothes, and when she tried to make a list of all she had to do before leaving, she found that most of the time she was sitting, pencil in hand, staring straight ahead at nothing, and imagining getting on to the huge aircraft and settling down for her long journey.

In no time at all it seemed she was

doing just that. Mr. Wentworth had approved of her move, and advanced the money for her ticket and other expenses. She attended to all the trivial details, paying her rent in advance, cancelling milk delivery and papers, and at the last minute, the turning off of the electricity, and water, against the danger of burst pipes should winter decide to linger a little longer in England. 'I'm going to the sun!' she kept whispering to herself like a magic incantation.

She spent an uncomfortable evening with Geoff, and blamed herself throughout for having suggested it. She had felt it would be unfair just to disappear without telling him, and so she had phoned and suggested a last meal together two days before her flight.

Geoff had been quiet and withdrawn, though he had obviously tried to enter into her enthusiastic discussion of her plans.

'When you come back, *if* you come back — ' he began once, and sensing that he was trying to tie her down to a promise that she might not want to keep, she had not let him finish.

'Oh, I don't think I'm going to disappear into Australia for ever,' she said gaily. 'If you like I'll write to you and we'll have another meal together when I get back.' Geoff obviously wanted much more than that, and Linda was touched as she watched his gallant attempts to match her excitement. Who knows, she thought, perhaps while I'm away I shall find that Geoff is the one person I want. Certainly since her mother's death he had been the most constant person in her life, and she had become very fond of him. It was hard to resist the impulse to take his large hand into hers and say, 'I'll come back to you, Geoff.' Several times she nearly did just that, but each time she realised afresh how new and how different everything was going to be. She wanted to be entirely free on this unexpected trip; not tied to her job nor to Geoff, and so the words were never spoken.

Clinton had helped her get a passport and had booked her a flight.

'Next Saturday at 11.52,' he told her, waving the ticket triumphantly when they met again for lunch as arranged. Her cheeks were pink with pleasure and anticipation.

'Have you sent a cable to Lance?' she asked.

'No. I thought it would be best to wait till nearer the time,' he replied. 'I'm supposed to phone Lance when all the paperwork is done. He's going to get quite a shock when he gets a cable instead, saying that you are arriving!'

Diana was silent. She felt uneasy at the thought of being unwelcome, but nothing was going to stop her now. She was going to Australia, going to Chickaroo, and going to find out all she could about the father she could never remember having seen, but who had nevertheless remembered her in his will.

5

Although, as Clinton had prophesied, it was almost midnight when her plane left Heathrow, Diana felt wide awake and alert. She had a window seat and continued to stare out of the window long after the lights of the airport had been left behind. Gradually blinds were drawn and lights extinguished. The stewardesses served drinks for a while, but soon even they were still, and Diana leaned back against the pillow she had been given, and dozed lightly.

She became aware of the first rustling movements of some fellow passengers, and soon she was sitting upright, all thoughts of sleep forgotten, and eager for what this new day would bring. She had never been in a plane before and was interested in everything that happened. She ate and enjoyed her breakfast from the neatly organised plastic tray, and felt a thrill of excitement as the Captain's voice announced the local time, and she put her watch forward three hours. Even the time is different, she thought, as she passed her tray to the stewardess and looked round at as many of her fellow passengers as she could. From their accents many were Australians returning home from some trip or other, but the elderly couple sitting next to her were English, and on their way to Australia for the first time to visit grand-children they had never seen. Photographs were produced and Diana admired the chunky little boy and smiling baby photographed on a beach. As the proud grandparents continued to give her details of the weight, height, beauty and intelligence of their son's children, Diana felt a pang of loneliness. When she had children what grandparents would they have? Supposing she married Geoff when her Australian visit was over? He had spoken of his parents often, but so far she had not met them.

Perhaps while she was away he would find someone else. It would be her own fault if he did, she thought; she had not wanted to be tied down to any promises yet — so why should he feel tied?

She put Geoff out of her mind and concentrated on enjoying the flight. During the morning she dozed again a little, but when some time after lunch, the captain announced that they would touch down at Melbourne in approximately two hours, she found herself looking out of the window and trying to will the time to pass more quickly. She tried to read but could not concentrate. The couple beside her sat silently; they had nothing more to say. They were interested only in their journey's end, and had asked no questions of Diana.

Slowly the time passed and at last she became aware that the plane was losing height. Seat belts were fastened and cigarettes extinguished, but still it seemed an age before there was anything to be seen below. As the wheels touched ground and the plane seemed to rush along the runway, Diana was aware only of bright sunlight and distant buildings. As the stewardess reminded everybody to make sure that they had their passports and landing cards ready, and that they left no personal belongings behind, there was a stirring amongst the passengers. Coats were lifted down, bags and packages collected and soon the aisle of the plane was full of standing figures all eager to disembark as quickly as possible.

Nearer to the airport buildings Diana became aware of waving figures on a balcony, and various passengers exclaimed 'I can see him!' or 'There they are!' She felt for the first time a little sense of misgiving. Clinton had sent the cable two days before she had left. It would be radioed to the station, he assured her, and Lance would be bound to meet her. Of course there had been no answer to the cable. She had not expected one, and in any case, what could an answer say? All the same she wondered how on earth she would manage to find Lance Ferguson among the seething mob of people waiting to meet passengers.

But of course I won't need to find him, she told herself; he'll find me. After all, he's only got to look for a girl travelling alone; it'll be much easier when some of the passengers have gone. Doubtfully she queued with everyone at Health and Immigration counters, and then waited for her luggage. She felt very alone as she stood silently listening to the crescendo of chatter around her. Her second suitcase was among the last to appear, and the crowd had thinned considerably, as, with a bag hanging from her shoulder, and a case in each hand, she walked slowly through the last barrier. Nobody seemed to look at her, and she wondered in sudden panic if it could be possible that Lance Ferguson had just ignored Clinton's cable. She walked across to an empty seat near the bookstall, and sat, with her cases at her feet, looking around.

There's no need to worry yet! she told

herself sternly; and indeed there was no need to worry at all, for within minutes a tall figure loomed over her, and an Australian drawl enquired, 'Would you be Miss Diana Barnes?'

She looked up into a pair of smiling grey eyes set in an incredibly brown face. He was tall, and his hair was as fair as Clinton's. Her heart lifted. 'Yes, I am,' she said. 'Are you Lance Ferguson?' The brown face crinkled into a wide smile.

'No, Miss. Lance — er — Lance couldn't get away. He sent me to fetch you. My name's Tim, Tim Lakett.' A huge brown hand enveloped hers, and for a second they just looked at each other. Then Diana gave a tiny sigh, and rose to her feet.

'I guess you're tired.' With one suitcase under his arm and the other in his hand, he put his free hand under her elbow and piloted her towards the exit. A taxi appeared at once as they stood by the kerb, and soon, with the luggage stowed in the boot they sat side by side on the back seat as the driver manipulated his car through the fast moving traffic.

'Mr. Lakett — '

'We'll be — ' they both began together.

'Please call me Tim,' he said quickly. 'We don't set much store on ceremony out at the station. Mrs. Blestow is the only one who has a handle to her name. I doubt if half of us even know the surnames of the other half.'

His drawling voice fascinated Diana, and she smiled back at him.

'You know my name is Diana,' she said.

'Ye — es; but the boss's daughter — '

'He's not the boss any more,' Diana reminded him gently, 'and Lance isn't called Mr. Ferguson.' Before her companion could reply she went on. 'How long have you been at Chickaroo? Did you know my father?'

'I've been there ten years, Miss — er — Diana,' he told her, 'and yes, I knew your father. He was a good man and a good boss. His death was a terrible shock to us all — as it must have been to you.' Diana did not answer the faint question in his voice. How, without being terribly disloyal to her mother's memory could she say that until recently she had always believed that her father had died eighteen years ago? Perhaps later, when she got to know Lance, she could tell him.

'Where are we going to now?' she asked instead.

'I've got us rooms in the hotel Lance always uses,' he told her. 'He thought that I might as well take back some supplies, as I'm here, and also that you might like to have a look round Melbourne before we go to the Outback. We'll leave the day after tomorrow.' Diana did not know what to say. Of course she was interested in seeing the city, but not now. Now she was eager to get to Chickaroo as soon as possible. Was it really necessary to get supplies? she wondered, or was Lance putting off as far as possible the moment when he would have to meet her and acknowledge her existence?

'I'd suggest that you have a kip right now.' Tim's voice broke into her speculations. 'You'll feel tired and in need of a shower after that long trip, I guess. I'll go and see about supplies, and meet you in the Lounge Bar of the hotel about eight for a meal and a drink. How's that?'

'That's fine,' she answered. 'Thank you.' However much Lance didn't want her, at least Tim was making her feel welcome, and she was grateful. Upstairs she realised that he was right, her initial alert excitement had given way to a feeling of tiredness. There was a bathroom adjoining her bedroom, and she revelled in a long, cool shower. Then, setting her alarm clock for seven-thirty, she slipped between smooth cotton sheets and was soon fast asleep. Thank goodness I brought an alarm clock, was her last conscious thought. With this terrific time change and the long journey, I might easily sleep on till morning.

So it would probably have been, for she seemed only to have been asleep for minutes when the shrill ringing summoned her back to her present surroundings. For a moment she lay feeling disorientated, and then she was on her feet and moving across to the window. She had not drawn the curtains and lights twinkled at her through the dark night. Quickly she drew them now, and rifled through her cases to find a crease resistant dress to wear. At five past eight she went down in the lift, and crossing the foyer, she found Tim waiting for her at the entrance to the bar.

'Sleep well?' he asked with a smile.

'Like a baby.' She smiled back. 'When the alarm rang I wondered where I was!'

Conversation was easy and pleasant during the meal, but Diana found that before it was finished she was sleepy again.

'I'm sorry!' she apologised after her second yawn. Her companion smiled understandingly.

'It's the long trip,' he told her. 'Your time has gone all wrong. You'll feel better after a good night's sleep. Come on. You'd better get upstairs before you fall asleep on me!'

'We really will be able to leave the day after tomorrow, won't we?' Diana asked when he had got her room key for her.

Tim smiled oddly.

'You're anxious to get there quickly, aren't you?'

'Yes. Yes — I am.'

'Why?'

His question surprised her and he read the surprise in her eyes as she looked up at him. 'I want to see where my father lived and meet all the people who knew him,' she answered.

'But you — ' he began and then stopped.

'But I what?'

'We could leave tomorrow afternoon if you like,' he said. 'The stores won't take long; but you won't see much of Melbourne.' Diana had the feeling that this was not what he had intended to say, but she was too pleased by the suggestion to question him further.

'I'd like that,' she said simply.

Tim nodded briefly.

'O.K. then. I'll have to leave you to your own resources in the morning. I'll get the goods hustled out to the plane, and we'll meet here for lunch at one and leave after that.'

'Thank you, Tim. That will be lovely, and thank you for dinner.'

'No thanks to me, girl. The boss pays.'

Diana flushed.

'I meant thank you for your company,' she retorted. 'The boss didn't provide me with his!'

'No — well — ' he said, looking uncomfortable.

'Well what?' Diana's growling dislike of Lance Ferguson and his high-handed attempts to avoid seeing her made her voice sharp.

'Well — we'll leave tomorrow afternoon,' Tim said lamely. Diana put a hand on his arm.

'I'm sorry,' she said. 'I didn't mean to be snappy. I just don't understand.'

Tim looked at her for a long moment, and she waited for him to speak.

'You shouldn't think badly of him, Diana,' he said uncomfortably. 'He loved your father. Although there was no blood relationship they were really like father and son, and he's been pretty upset.' There seemed no easy answer to this, so Diana said goodnight and, watched by Tim with an unfathomable look in his eyes, she crossed to the lift.

As she prepared for bed her heart was full of conflicting emotions. Maybe Lance is very upset about my father's death, she thought, but that is not my fault; and after all he did have eighteen years of having a father, while I had none that I can remember. In spite of her churning thoughts and feelings, she fell asleep quickly and woke refreshed to another day of brilliant sunshine.

After a breakfast which appalled her by its vast quantity, she wandered out and around the streets, fascinated by everything she saw, and by the cheerful babble of talk everywhere, which sounded sometimes almost like another language. She kept an eye on her watch and was back at the hotel in time to have a refreshing shower and change her dress before going down to meet Tim. He was waiting as he had been the evening before, and he greeted her with a smile.

'Everything's done,' he told her cheerfully, 'and as soon as we've had a meal we'll go out to the air field.'

'I wonder if I'll be able to eat a thing;' Diana said. 'They gave me such a huge breakfast.'

'Australian breakfasts are usually pretty substantial,' Tim told her. 'You can just have a light lunch. You mustn't upset Mrs. Blestow by not eating the first meal of your stay, which will be dinner tonight.'

'I'll have to watch it, or I'll be putting on weight,' she replied lightly; but resentfully she thought, Why do I have to worry about upsetting the housekeeper? No one seems to worry about upsetting me!

After lunch her cases were once more put into a taxi, and soon she was standing with Tim beside a small plane. After the jumbo jet which had brought her to Australia it seemed like a toy, and Diana eyed it apprehensively. Tim mistook her expression for one of admiration, and beamed his approval.

'Beautiful, isn't she?' he said. 'The boss always did the best he could for the station. Not like some who spend all the profits in city life as soon as they get them. He had a good life as the station grew, but it must have been very difficult in the beginning putting everything he gained back into the station.'

'It — it must be very useful to have,' Diana heard herself reply lamely.

'Useful? I'll say it is! It's a long trip by road. We have a chopper, too, as well as this Cessna. It's a damn shame the boss didn't live to enjoy it all more,' he ended on a harsher note. Diana was silent.

'Well, come on. I'll help you in.' Tim's lazy drawl had returned, and soon they were airborne, and after Diana's first moments of fear as the tiny plane took off, she settled down to enjoy the ride. They flew low, and Tim pointed out mountains and valleys in the distance, and named some sheep stations they passed on their journey north-eastwards. Diana murmured what she hoped were appropriate noises, but her whole being was absorbed with the thought that soon she would be at her journey's end.

'Any minute now we'll be there!' Tim told her, raising his voice above the noise of the plane. Diana kept her eyes on the land ahead, determined not to miss the first sight of the station, but they were circling round it and Tim suddenly touched her arm and pointed downwards on the left. 'There!' he said.

Looking eagerly down, all Diana could see at first was a cluster of buildings and a plumed trail of dust as someone evidently drove a car towards them. As the plane circled again and dropped lower, she was able to see the different buildings, and Tim pointed and explained. 'The big house is over there, with the lubras' quarters behind it. That's the bunkhouse over there — that long, low building.'

'The one that looks L-shaped?' Diana asked.

'Too right!' Tim's accent seemed even stronger now. 'The long bit is where we sleep and the shorter bit is the kitchen-dining room and games room.'

'The place seems very well equipped.'

'Sure is! The boss provided real good conditions and he was able to get his pick of workers.'

'The lubras?'

'They're aborigine women,' Tim answered the question in her voice. 'We've got four. They make good workers, better than the men, though we do have one old abo gardener who somehow grows us wonderful vegetables. Living out so far, fresh food is something of a rarity on most stations, except for lamb and mutton that is — but we do pretty well.'

By this time the plane was coming in to land, and Diana felt her palms wet with excitement and apprehension. As the little plane taxied to a standstill, she saw the jeep driving out to meet them. Now at last I'll meet Mr. Lance Ferguson! she thought. But she was wrong. Tim helped her down from the plane, the jeep drew up and a grizzled man of about fifty got out of it.

'This is Joe, our handyman.' Tim said. 'Joe, meet Miss Diana, the boss's daughter.' After a second's hesitation the man offered her a gnarled brown hand. 'Good day, Miss Diana,' he said.

'Take us to the house, will you, Joe?' Tim said. 'And then come back for the stuff. We'll take Miss Diana's cases with us.'

Soon they were standing on the verandah of the long, low house, and Joe was going back to the Cessna.

'Come inside, and I'll fetch Mrs.

Blestow,' Tim urged, but before he could even pick up the cases, a middle-aged woman came out to meet them.

'I heard the plane circling,' she said disapprovingly. 'Lance said you were to come back tomorrow.'

'Yes.' Tim agreed. 'But Diana was anxious to get here as soon as may be, so I got everything fixed up this morning.' The woman did not reply, and he went on almost placatingly, 'after all she can see Melbourne any time,' he said, 'and the whole purpose of her journey was to come here.'

'Well, yes, I suppose so. She can stay in the city on her way back.' Then addressing herself to the girl, she said, 'Come in, Miss Barnes. I'll get a lubra to make some tea while I show you your room.'

'You must be Mrs. Blestow,' Diana said, offering her hand, 'and please call me Diana.' The woman shook her hand briefly, and as she turned to lead the way, she said over her shoulder — 'Tim, you'd better let Lance know you're here. He's over at the dip — overseeing some repairs. Come along, Miss Diana.' The girl looked back, too, and Tim raised his hand in farewell.

'See you later!' he smiled.

'This way,' Mrs. Blestow told her, and Diana turned to follow her with a ridiculous sense of having been abandoned to the enemy. Mrs. Blestow seemed certainly to be the dragon that Clinton had said she was, and Diana hoped that everyone received the same cavalier treatment, and that the housekeeper was not being especially churlish to her.

She was led to a charming room with its own bathroom and a French window leading to the verandah which ran all round the house.

'You'll want to wash and change, I expect,' her guide assumed. 'I'll have some tea sent to you here. Dinner is at eight, but I'll have a lubra fetch you before then to show you where to go.'

'Thank you — ' Diana began, but the

woman was already outside the door, and Diana sat down on the side of the bed, feeling suddenly like a child who has been sent to its room for some misdemeanour.

6

She explored her bedroom and bathroom, which were opulent by the
standards of her flat in England.
Everything was in varying shades of
green which gave the place a cool look,
despite the blazing sun outside. The
curtains and cover of the double bed
matched, and the towels and tiles in the
bathroom were a different shade of
green. The triple mirror on the dressing
table gave a sudden three dimensional
vision of herself. How pale she looked
compared with everyone else she had
seen! Her eyes seemed larger than ever,
and she felt discontented with the
slightly waif-like look of her face. Her
hair was untidy, her dress rumpled and
her shoes dusty. No wonder Mrs.
Blestow assumed I'd want to wash and
change! She thought ruefully. Her
humour over-rode her annoyance. Well,

I will! I came to see Chickaroo, and that's what I'll do — and nobody's going to put me off!

An hour later, showered and dressed in a pink dress (uncrushable, thank goodness!) which made her look less waif-like, she sat in front of the triple mirror and applied make-up to her eyes and mouth. At home, she used little make-up, often forgetting to use it at all, but now she was glad that she had brought some with her. She was certainly not going to meet Lance Ferguson looking pale and tired! For some reason it seemed, he resented her very existence, and, quite contrary to her normal character, she found herself thinking. If he wants a fight he can have one! I'm not going to give him chance to feel sorry for me for any reason! She herself realised that this was perhaps rather muddled thinking, but her pride had been touched by the obvious lack of welcome, and a well made-up face and trimly dressed figure seemed at the moment, like armour necessary for battle. Unfortunately, being unused to make-up, the finished result did not please her. She had rubbed rouge around her cheek bones, hoping to hide the pallor of nerves and tiredness from the long journey, and the result looked rather like a painted Dutch doll she had once owned. Her lipstick was over-red for the pink dress, and the black mascara made her eyes sting. She was looking at herself with rueful amusement when a discreet tap at the door heralded a dark girl in a green dress.

'You come along now, Miss. I show you.' For a moment Diana hesitated, wanting to ask the girl to wait while she removed the make-up and re-washed her face, but her natural disinclination for making a purposely late entry won, and obediently she stood up and prepared to follow the lubra. She was led along a wide, carpeted passage to a room off the big entrance hall. At the door the lubra stood back to let Diana enter. With what she told herself was a ridiculous clenching of her hands by her sides and trembling of her knees, she did so. A small group of men sat with glasses in their hands, and as one man they rose to their feet as she entered. She was relieved to see that Tim was among them, and he came forward to greet her.

'Since I met you first, I'll do the honours,' he said, and taking her hand he led her forward. For a moment the figures seemed to swim in a haze, before she became aware of blazing blue eyes looking her up and down and taking in every detail of her dress, figure, and — she felt sure, unfortunate — make-up.

'This is Diana, Lance,' Tim said, and the girl was at once uncomfortably aware that she was being presented to the man, and not he to her.

'Diana, this is Lance Ferguson,' Tim said belatedly, and to Diana's amazement, there was a sudden hush as they confronted each other. Nervousness made her speak first.

'So at last I meet you,' she said, rather

more loudly than she had intended, and before Lance could make any reply except a slight tightening of his lips, she turned again to Tim.

'Won't you introduce me to the others?' Embarrassedly, he did so.

'This is Charlie,' he said, and Diana extended her hand with a smile.

'I'm pleased to meet you,' she smiled.

'How do you do, Miss Diana?'

'This is Barney, who keeps all our machinery including the plane and chopper, working so well,' Tim went on.

'Pleased to meet you, Miss Diana.'

'Hallo, Barney. It's the first time I'd travelled in such a small plane,' she told him, taking his hand. The man smiled but made no answer.

'And last, and definitely least,' Tim grinned, 'here's Johnnie, who's supposed to be learning about sheep-farming.' The young man, who Diana guessed, was about her own age, blushed slightly, but put out his hand and welcomed her more whole-heartedly than anyone else had done.

'Hello, Diana,' he grinned. 'May I call you Diana? Everyone goes by first names here except Mrs. Blestow. You're like manna from heaven. It seems years since I saw an attractive girl.' Diana felt a wave of gratitude and she held his hand firmly, smiling into his face. Before she had a chance to answer, however, Lance spoke.

'Talking of Blessie, where is she? Go and see, will you, Johnnie? And Tim, get Diana a drink.'

Everyone sat down again as the boy left the room. Tim dragged up a chair for Diana, and asked her what she would like to drink, while Lance carried on with the conversation he had been engaged in, and took no further notice of her. Tim brought her a glass of sherry and was about to sit beside her when Lance called him over. Diana's hand tightened round the stem of her glass. The man was being deliberately rude and she felt humiliated and helpless. She took a sip of her drink and tried to relax. She would just wait. Surely he wouldn't be able to keep up this behaviour all the time? She glanced round at the other faces. There had been a great deal of reserve in their greeting, too, she thought, or was she just tired, over-excited and over-imaginative? Johnnie's entry with the housekeeper put an end to her thoughts, as the men once more rose to their feet.

'Where've you been, Blessie? We missed you.' Lance took a step forward, his smile completely transforming his severe, blue-eyed, brown face.

Mrs. Blestow stood woodenly and looked back at him.

'I thought things might be different now, Mr. Lance,' she said, without even a glance in Diana's direction. 'I was seeing to the dinner.'

'Blessie, don't be silly.' His tone was affectionate as he crossed to put an arm around her shoulders. 'We all know that you've got your lubras so well-trained that you never need 'to see to the dinner'. You're always here to eat with us and have a drink with us first! What'll it be? The usual?' But Mrs. Blestow was not going to unbend easily.

'If I'm still to eat with you I must get another place laid,' she told him, turning to go.

'Oh, no, you don't!' Lance's arm tightened around her ample form. 'Johnnie, tell the lubras to lay another place.' As the boy stood up Lance went on, 'Nothing has changed, Blessie. You will continue to join us, and to sit at the foot of the table as you have always done since my mother died.' Surreptitiously several pairs of eyes slid towards Diana. Lance's words had been such an obvious challenge that she could not ignore it. She cast aside her decision just to wait, and raised her voice slightly, looking quickly around the room and then letting her gaze linger on the housekeeper. 'We all know, I'm sure, that it's not quite true that nothing has changed,' she said, marvelling to herself that her voice did not tremble, 'but I would not like to be the cause of depriving you all of Mrs. Blestow's company, nor of depriving her of her place at the table.' Ignoring the almost tangible hush, she and Lance looked into each other's eyes. His were furious and hers stubborn. Well, that's it, she was thinking. I can't for the life of me think why, but a challenge has been thrown down and accepted. I wonder what he'll do now?

Whatever she expected, Lance was evidently not going to retort at once or in public. Instead he laughed, which was as infuriating as any reply could have been.

'There you are, Blessie,' he said. 'Nothing is going to change! Now sit down and I'll get you that drink.' He did not look at Diana as he crossed to the drinks cabinet, but she had to admit to herself that in this ridiculous battle, the first round had definitely gone to Lance. He had laughed away her attempt to annoy, and he had made a point of going himself to get Mrs. Blestow's drink instead of ordering the boy to do so.

As conversation broke out again Johnnie stood beside her. Diana recklessly drained her glass. 'Will you get me another, please?' she asked, and tried to control the trembling of her hands as he handed her the refilled glass and took the empty chair next to hers. His puzzled look showed that he was aware of some tension, but he did not understand it.

'She scares me to death,' he said in a low, conspiratorial voice. 'And isn't it odd, Lance is the only one who doesn't call her Mrs. Blestow, yet she always calls him Mr. Lance?'

Diana smiled, relaxing a little.

'I believe she's been here always,' she said. 'Old habits die hard. He probably called her Blessie when he was a child, and she's always called him 'Mr. Lance'. She paused, then went on. 'Did my father call her 'Blessie', too?' she asked.

Johnnie shook his head.

'I don't know. I've only been here a month,' he told her. 'Usually two students come together to a station, but

112

this time there was only me. I hope you are going to stay a long time. It'll be wonderful just to see someone about my own age.'

'Some of the men can't be much older than you surely?'

'Maybe not in age, but in experience, vastly so. They've more or less grown up to station work, and I've come straight from college. I get a lot of ribbing about it, too, I can tell you. Not when Lance is about. He grew up in the station *and* went to college, so he knows the value of both.'

'Were there two students here before you?' Diana asked.

'No. I'm the first one to come to this station. Lance's stepfather didn't go much for the idea. It's one of the changes Lance has made. I'm not sure it's too popular with the men, though most of them are good sorts, even if they do tease me a lot.'

'I can see how it would be better for two of you,' Diana said, 'and *I* am very glad that you're here, because I know absolutely nothing!' Before he could answer there was a stir as everyone got to their feet to walk through to the adjacent dining room. Mrs. Blestow evidently knew from some remote sign that dinner was now ready.

As Tim had said, the food was excellent; well-cooked and served in abundance. Diana ate and drank, but afterwards she could not have said what. Seven of them sat at the table, and whether by design or accident, Diana found herself sitting on Lance's right. Apparently it was an unspoken rule that no one talked shop at meal times. Conversation was general, and hanging on to her dwindling burst of courage, Diana joined in whenever she could.

'How was Clint enjoying himself among the pommies?' Tim asked her in a sudden silence.

'He's permanently cold,' she replied, and spurred on by the general laugh which followed, she described how he had been wrapped up in sweaters and a furlined coat, and still complaining of the cold. Talk switched to neighbours. 'Jake's back on Burrowlee,' Barney told Tim. 'I spoke to him on the radio this morning.'

'Jake's our nearest neighbour, only seventy miles away,' Tim explained to Diana. 'The radio doctor had to get him into hospital quickly with a burst appendix.'

'Seems like he's recovering quickly,' Barney added. 'He sounded fighting fit this morning. He's sending our two boys back.'

'Lance sent two of our men to help out while he was away,' Johnnie put in.

'Will you have some more wine, Diana?' Lance asked, cutting short any comment she might have made.

'Yes, please.' She held out her glass. Normally she drank very little, and though she was well aware that tonight she was perhaps drinking too much, it gave her a warm feeling, and seemed to help her to carry on with this interminable meal. 'Australian wines are very good,' she added, as Lance filled her glass.

'Are you a wine connoisseur?' he asked smoothly and she flushed.

'No. I like wine, but I haven't experienced much. It's just that one tends to think that the Continent produces good wine, and it's a pleasant surprise to find that Australia does, too.'

'You mean the continent of Europe?' Barney asked.

'Yes. I suppose we — we pommies — tend to think of it as *the* Continent, when of course it's one of several.'

'Seven,' Johnnie said.

'Watch it, boy. Your education's showing!' Charlie commented, and all joined in the laughter.

'I'm glad it does sometimes!' Johnnie retorted as he, too, laughed. 'Mostly I feel so ignorant.'

'You'll learn,' Lance said in a kindly voice, making Johnnie blush with pleasure. Made bold by the wine, Diana looked directly at Lance. 'I can't believe I'm really here at last,' she said. 'I'm

116

longing to see and learn about everything.'

He looked at her for a moment in silence, an unfathomable look in his blue eyes.

'That's a tall order,' he said at last. 'It's a big station, I don't suppose you'll be here long enough to see everything; and learning everything, as anyone here will tell you, is almost impossible. Even after years there's something new to learn.'

Diana could find no answer. He had taken her remark so literally. She sat silently and Johnnie came to her rescue.

'That's true,' he said. 'I've been here a month, and I've only really learned that you don't do as you're told and go and ask somebody for a sack of pot-holes, or really believe that Mrs. Blestow wants me to peel potatoes.' Even Mrs. Blestow joined in the laughter this time.

'I'm well-organised,' she protested. 'I certainly wouldn't want any of you great men getting in the way in my kitchen.'

'Well anyway, it's nice to know that

one person regards me as a great man!' the boy retorted.

'Yes. You'll be promoted now,' Lance put in smoothly. 'I want you to give up your day to Diana tomorrow. Ask Blessie to pack you a lunch, and you can show Diana as much as you can in a day's ride. Charlie — get one of the men to saddle up something suitable.'

'How good a rider are you, Diana?' Charlie asked. Linda could think of no reply but the truth.

'I — I've never been on a horse in my life,' she blurted out. Lance's sigh was audible only to her.

'In that case,' he said, 'saddle up something quiet, Charlie, and you' — he looked at Johnnie — 'can start to teach her to ride.'

He turned at once to speak to Barney on his other side, and Diana sat flushed and dejected.

At last the meal was over and the soft-footed lubras appeared to clear the table. Mrs. Blestow bade everyone goodnight, and went off to her own quarters. 'Breakfast is any time from six on, Miss Diana,' she said, as a parting shot, 'but I don't suppose you're used to getting up that early.'

'I'll be ready whenever Johnnie wants me,' said the girl quietly.

'If we have breakfast at seven it'll be fine.' Johnnie told her. Then he, too, said goodnight and went off. The others were dispersing as well, and Diana felt that she was being tidied away like the wrapping on a parcel.

'I'd — I'd like to talk to you about — about everything,' she said to Lance, and his eyebrows rose just a fraction.

'I'm sure you would,' he agreed, 'but I have work to do tonight and as you've come to see the station, maybe you'd better do that before we talk.'

'It's not necessary — ' she began, and he interrupted her.

'I wouldn't have thought so,' he agreed, 'but here you are. I'm pretty busy, but after today I'll try to make myself available to talk whenever you want.'

Diana glanced at her watch as the tall figure left the room. It was a little after half past nine, much too early to go to bed. Yet even Johnnie had half-apologetically followed the others. She wondered if they always dispersed like this after the meal, or if when her father had been alive he and Lance had gone back to the drawing-room or out on to the verandah to sit and chat in the warm night air. Shrugging her shoulders slightly she went slowly back along the passage to her room. Someone — one of the lubras she supposed — had put a caraffe of water and a sparkling glass on her bedside table, and had turned down the bedclothes and laid out her nightdress. Mrs. Blestow certainly had a well-trained staff. What a lot she would have had to learn if she had been going to stay and make her home here! Tonight she felt tired and depressed; the temporary exhilaration brought by the wine had evaporated, and she almost wished she had not come. Why *did* Lance resent her so much? For there was now no doubt that he did. She opened the French window in her bedroom and stepped out on to the verandah. Some distance away, she would see the lights of the men's quarters, and across the still air she could hear music and cheerful voices. The stars seemed very low in the sky, and an almost full moon made the distant hills look theatrically lovely. Some wild animal gave a yelping bark, and she shivered slightly and went inside. Johnnie, the boy, seemed the only person willing to talk uninhibitedly with her, and he had not known her father.

Dispiritedly she prepared for bed. Her clothes, she noticed, had been unpacked and put away, and her suitcases had disappeared. No doubt the efficient Mrs. Blestow had some place where they were kept out of the way until needed again. And no doubt, she told herself gloomily, she hopes it'll be soon!

As she hung up her dress and put out

a shirt and a pair of jeans ready for the next day, her spirits lifted a little. After all, she thought, I *am* here. My father did remember me and want me to share the station. I owe it to him at least not to back out and go meekly home.

Tomorrow she would be with Johnnie, and he was a cheerful companion. Although he said he'd learned very little in his first month, he would be able to tell her a great deal about sheep stations in general, *and* he was going to teach her to ride. She would learn quickly, she determined, and tired out with the day's emotions and events, she fell quickly asleep to dream of galloping horses and flocks of very white, woolly sheep.

She woke early next morning without the aid of her alarm clock, and could not help but feel happy as she saw what a beautiful morning it was. The dining room was empty, but there was a fine array of food on hot chafing dishes and a hovering lubra came forward as she entered.

'You like tea or you like coffee, Miss?'

She asked with a flashing of white teeth.

'Coffee, please,' Diana told her, and was just helping herself to toast and marmalade when Johnnie walked in.

'Hullo — good morning!' he greeted her cheerfully. 'I see you are properly dressed for riding. Gosh — is that all you're having for breakfast?'

'And coffee,' she told him smiling.

'If you stay in Australia long you'll soon learn to eat big breakfasts,' Johnnie predicted as he helped himself to sausages, tomatoes and two chops. Diana looked at his plate in pretended horror. 'How *can* you eat all that and stay so thin?'

'We don't have time for mid-morning snacks,' he said seriously. 'You need a good hearty breakfast to set you up for the morning's work.'

'I hope I'll be a good pupil,' Diana said, suddenly serious.

'I've never actually taught anyone to ride,' he told her. 'I suppose I can only teach you roughly what to do, and how to handle horses. That's the worst of being a new boy! You get all the jobs no one else wants.' His ready blush stained his face as he realised what he had said. 'I — I didn't mean that,' he protested. 'I'll be glad to have your company. It's just that I don't know how good a teacher I shall be.'

He turned out to be a good teacher, and a teacher with a very exacting pupil, for Diana insisted on keeping on and on, until at last, tired and sore, she had made enough progress to suit herself.

7

During the days of her riding lessons with Johnnie, Diana did not feel so isolated. He could not tell her anything except hearsay about her father but he could and did, tell her everything he had already learned about the station, and he showed her everything within easy riding distance.

'Lance wants to expand the vegetable growing,' he told her one day. 'In the old — in your father's time, just enough for home consumption was grown. Of course, transport is a problem, but the ground is good, and Lance reckons that in the long run it would pay.' He chattered happily, glad of the companionship of his own age, and glad, for a while, to be the teacher instead of the pupil. Diana questioned him avidly, but in all that she gleaned from his answers she could find no reason for the definite coolness with which she was treated by everyone, and particularly by Lance. It could be that the men and Mrs. Blestow took their lead from him, but why should *he* be so antagonistic? Everything she learnt about him showed Lance to be a mature man, friendly and considerate with his employees, yet firm and unmoving about the carrying out of his orders, even if they did go against established tradition. Surely such a man — however disappointed he may have been to find out that he was not now sole owner of Chickaroo — would have come to terms with the fact by now, accepted it, and be making the best of it? There was nothing that could be accomplished by treating her as if she were an unwanted and unwelcome stranger. Of course I *am* a stranger, she reminded herself, but not of my own choosing.

All too soon, however, she had to lose Johnnie's company. At dinner one night Lance made the crimson blush flood Diana's face by ignoring her completely, as he said to Johnnie, 'Anyone should have been able to learn to ride by now. So unless you're an exceptionally bad teacher, you'd better get back to your own jobs again. If Diana wants to ride, anyone who is about can saddle up the mare for her, and see to it when she's finished.'

With a little spurt of temper the girl intervened. 'I can do it myself.'

Lance looked at her.

'Very well,' he agreed calmly, 'but let one of the men make sure you do it properly before you take it upon yourself to do it all alone.' Ignoring her then, he turned and began to talk to Mrs. Blestow.

Swallowing her chagrin, Diana turned away, too, and thanked Johnnie for the time he had given her, and how much he had taught her. 'I only hope I'll be a credit to you,' she smiled.

'You're doing fine,' he told her. 'I only wish you weren't!' She was aware of Tim's tolerant smile from the other side of the table.

'Hard luck, boy,' he said. 'No more goofing off! Back to real hard work tomorrow.' Diana flushed, but did not answer.

'Yes. I've been keeping you from all you should be learning', she smiled, trying to smooth over the teasing. Johnnie looked at her silently, and she felt a little awkward under his intent gaze. Thankfully she answered the questions Tim began to ask her about England. He's kind, she thought. He seems to be the only one, except Johnnie, who is willing to stick his neck out and talk to me. The others answer politely enough if I speak to them, but that's about all. Sometimes, she told herself, she felt like an unwanted child at a party. Everyone else was dutifully polite to her, but nobody really wanted her there. When talk at the table became general, she sat like someone invisible, and watched and listened. No one ever drew her into the conversation or asked her opinion about whatever it was they happened to be discussing. It's all his doing, she thought resentfully, glaring at Lance. But even if he resents me, as well he might, I don't understand why everyone should so slavishly copy him.

Looking round suddenly, Lance caught her eye.

'Did you say something?' he asked.

'No.' The monosyllable was abrupt, but instead of making any comment he just turned away and began talking to the man on his other side. Diana's lips compressed angrily, and she determined that she would force some kind of a showdown in an attempt to find the cause of Lance's attitude. Every evening after dinner he had disappeared with the other men, and she had either sat uncomfortably in the drawing room with the housekeeper, who silently knitted, read, or wrote letters, or she had gone early to her room. In the first days, tired out and stiff, she had been glad to take a hot bath and go to bed early, but now she felt happy and at ease on a horse, and although pleasantly tired each day, she had no wish to continue to disappear after dinner as everyone else did; nor had she any wish to sit in silence with Mrs. Blestow.

As they left the table and a few goodnights were said, Diana put herself in front of Lance. 'I'd like to talk to you,' she said firmly. His eyebrows rose a fraction, but his expression did not change.

'Talk away,' he invited. Diana breathed deeply. 'Not here,' she said. Lance looked around. 'Where would you like to talk then?' he asked, as if humouring a child.

'If Miss Diana wants to be private, I can go to my room,' Mrs. Blestow offered, as she paused in the doorway.

'Of course not,' Lance dismissed the suggestion. 'Why should you leave? We'll go to my office.' He turned and walked down the passageway, leaving Diana to follow him like a child. Angrily she did so. At the door of his office he stood back to let her enter and she stood there uncertainly till he indicated a chair and said 'Please sit down.' For a moment she thought he would sit behind his desk as if interviewing an employee, and her fists clenched involuntarily, but he took an armchair opposite hers, and fumbled in his pocket for his pipe as he said. 'Well?'

For a moment she was silent, trying to find the right words, but Lance interrupted her thoughts. 'You want to talk about the station and your inheritance,' he stated. 'Well — '

'And about my father, and — '

'I don't want to talk about your father,' Lance said with an odd note in his voice, 'but I can tell you anything you want to know about the station, and as soon as — '

Diana interrupted this time.

'Why don't you want to talk about my father?' she demanded.

Again those maddening eyebrows rose as he looked at her. For a second he held her angry gaze and then his eyes dropped as he occupied himself with filling his pipe.

'I can't imagine why you want to

131

know anything about Charles,' he said in a forced, even tone, 'but in any case I don't intend to talk about him. I'm sure the will has been read to you and you know therefore that he left everything to be divided equally between us. It's going to take a little while, and be a bit difficult to determine exactly what half is worth, and now today there's been another hindrance; but in any case, surely you could have been a bit patient about it? You won't get the money any sooner by coming out here yourself.'

'I don't care about the money,' she interrupted passionately.

Lance's mouth hardened as he looked across at her, and his answering voice, in comparison to hers, was like ice.

'I find that extremely difficult to believe,' he said, his knuckles white as he clutched the unlit pipe. 'But even if it were true, the estate has to be divided. That is what Charles wanted and that is what will be done.'

'But you resent having to lose half the station, don't you?' she flashed back.

'On the contrary. Charles gave me everything while he was alive. The station was his, and, as far as I am concerned he was welcome to do whatever he liked with it. He loved me like a son, and treated me like one; and I loved him. He didn't need to leave me anything to prove his love, but as he has, I will continue to run the station and improve it as I know he would want.'

Diana looked at him. His face looked strained and he obviously found it painful to talk about the stepfather he had so recently lost; but Charles had been her father, too, and he had wanted her to inherit, so why was Lance so antagonistic? On impulse she reached out her hand to him.

'I'm sure you must miss him very much, Lance,' she said, warm sympathy in her voice, 'but why are you so unfriendly?'

'I'm not unfriendly. I'm indifferent,' he told her coldly. 'I just want to get the whole matter settled, and bid you goodbye.' He pointedly ignored her outstretched hand, and, feeling rather foolish, she returned it to clasp the other in her lap. His eyes followed her movement, and remained on her hands while she vainly tried to think of something else to say.

Lance seemed visibly to control himself before he spoke again.

'You are quite right,' he said in a cold even voice. 'You are not welcome here; there is no need for you to be here. As soon as it is possible to do so, I will get the accounts audited, and arrangements made for a settlement. Unfortunately that will have to be postponed for a little while. I heard from Clinton today that he's had an accident and broken a leg and his collarbone, so his return will be delayed, and obviously I would like the books to be as up-to-date as possible before I call in the auditors, but I can assure you that there is no need for you to remain. Everything will be done just as soon as it is possible.'

Diana was silent. The thought of

leaving was painful. She realised suddenly that however unwelcome she had been made, she infinitely preferred being here to being in England. She loved the weather, the way of life, all the new things she was seeing and learning; even the isolation. The men, too, she knew, were interesting, each in his own way, if only they would condescend to do more than merely answer her questions! But it seemed that they took their lead from Lance, the new boss, and it seemed that he could not be persuaded to regard her in a more favourable light.

He was about to get to his feet, terminating this unsatisfactory interview, when the idea came to her.

'Lance, I'm an accountant,' she said impulsively. 'Could I take over till Clinton is able to come back? I'd — I'd like to help.'

He stood up and paused, looking down at her.

'You *are* in a hurry to get everything settled,' he said cuttingly. 'Well, that suits me, too. The sooner everything's settled the sooner you can leave. Now, if you'll excuse me I'm going to — '

Diana, too, was on her feet.

'It's not that!' she cried. 'I just thought it was something I could do — to help. Everyone is working except for me.'

Lance held the door open for her.

'Whatever the reason,' he said drily, 'I accept your offer. Maybe that way we'll both get what we want.'

Diana felt tears sting her eyes.

'You don't know what I want,' she protested with a sob in her voice. 'You won't let me — '

'If you'll meet me here at ten tomorrow,' Lance interrupted, 'I'll take you to Clinton's little office and show you the books and so on.' With trembling knees Diana walked past him and heard the door close firmly behind her. She stumbled along the passage half-blinded by tears, and in her own room she flung herself on the bed and let the tears come.

After a long time she got up wearily and prepared for bed. What did it matter, after all, she asked herself, whether Lance were friendly or not? She had seen the station now, and learned a bit about it. Enough, she knew, to wish that she could stay much longer. As for Lance, well — but even as these thoughts went through her tired mind, she realised, and had to admit to herself, that Lance's unfriendliness did matter. She had seen him teasing Mrs. Blestow, giving curt, clear but friendly orders to the men, gently pulling the ears of the housedog which ran to greet him, and filling his pocket with sugar lumps for his horse. To everyone except her, it seemed, he was warm and friendly, and she felt hurt and isolated. Now, impulsively she had offered to do something that she thought would help him, only to have her motives crudely misinterpreted. She *would* leave. What was the point in staying any longer? Tomorrow she would tell Lance that she wanted to get back to Melbourne as soon as possible. She had not much money left, but no doubt he would be only too glad to advance her enough to stay in the city while she arranged a return flight.

With such bitter thoughts she fell asleep and dreamed of riding fast on the mare she had come to think of as her own, in a vain attempt to catch a small plane, which, oddly, seemed to grow bigger and bigger.

She awoke unrefreshed, to the ever-new thrill of seeing bright sunlight pouring in at the bedroom window. It was early, she knew without looking at her watch. A little later the sun would rise above the verandah roof, and the house would be cool and shady. She slipped out of bed, completely forgetting her plans to leave. She had till ten. She would saddle the mare, and ride before breakfast.

In jeans and a white shirt she crossed to the stables. The mare she rode and one other were still there. No doubt the men were working already and had either taken food with them or would return at ten-thirty for breakfast. Quickly she saddled the mare, remembering all she had been taught, and soon they were trotting along, both of them enjoying the morning. How different from all that her life had been so far! There had been a heavy dew and a million sparkles made the ground look diamond-strewn. Far ahead she could see the gleam of the River Murrumbidgee. Later she knew that it would join the many other tributaries and flow down to the sea east of Adelaide. The river seemed to beckon her and she abandoned herself to the enjoyment of the ride, thinking only of the moment and nothing of the past or future. After a while pangs of hunger made her turn back, and when she glanced at her watch she found that she had taken longer and had come further than she realised. She would have to hurry and probably go without breakfast, too, in order to meet Lance at ten.

She kicked the mare into a canter and

not at all unwilling to return, she lengthened her stride obediently. The pace was exhilarating, and, unconsciously Diana urged her to more and more speed. Suddenly she seemed to hear a shout behind her, and half-turned in her saddle to see who it was. She was not yet an experienced enough rider, and the movement unbalanced her; in vain she clutched at the saddle; she was just in time to see Lance galloping up behind her before she fell heavily to the ground. The wind was knocked from her body, and she was momentarily unconscious before she became aware of a rough arm lifting her shoulders, and an equally rough voice saying. 'You little fool! You might have broken your neck!' His face was close to hers, and his strong arm felt infinitely comforting.

'Perhaps then at last I should have done something to please you,' she murmured.

His face came closer to hers.

'Nothing you could do would please

me!' he said savagely. 'You are a thorn in my flesh.' Before she had time even to wonder what he meant, his lips were pressed hard on hers, and his arm tightened about her shoulders. She felt herself responding to the demands of his mouth, and her arm crept up to go round his neck. Then, with startling abruptness he released her, leaving only one arm stiffly behind her so that she did not fall. She glanced up at him and was surprised to see his face harden like a mask.

'I apologise,' he said curtly. 'I shouldn't have done that.'

'But, Lance — ' she was bewildered.

'I'll help you up,' he told her, equally curtly. 'Let's see if you can ride back.' Diana's thoughts were in chaos. How sweet it had been — that kiss. She knew suddenly and without any doubt that she had fallen in love with this curt, unfriendly man. It was more than his friendship and acceptance she wanted and for those few wonderful moments it had seemed that he was showing her he felt that way, too. Now suddenly the atmosphere between them was as chilly as it had always been.

'How do you feel?' he asked, as with trembling hands she brushed the dust from her jeans.

A thousand answers sprang to her lips, but she only said woodenly, 'I'm all right.'

He held the mare while she mounted, and silently and slowly they rode back to Chickaroo. Once or twice she glanced sideways at his stern, set face, but he kept his eyes straight ahead. Only when they reached the corral and dismounted, did he look at her again.

'Go back to bed,' he instructed her. 'You may have concussed yourself and you'd better lie still for a while. I'll see to the horses.'

'I'm all right.' Her curt voice matched his. 'I'm going to work on the accounts, remember?'

For a second his eyes blazed. 'You will do as I say. The accounts can wait one more day. You'll be even more of a nuisance if you're ill.'

The cruel words were at such variance with his kiss that she stared at him, shocked, before turning blindly away and hurrying to her bedroom.

With shaking fingers she undressed and crept into bed where she lay, shivering slightly, in spite of the warmth. She lay on her back and stared at the ceiling. I will leave, she thought, as she seemed to hear him say again, 'You'll be even more of a nuisance.' Obviously in spite of that strange kiss, his attitude towards her was not going to change. She pondered her newly-awoken feelings for him. How could she have fallen in love with him, cold and arrogant as he was? Yet she knew without any shadow of doubt that she had. She longed for his hands to be as gentle with her as they were with his horse and the old dog. She longed to hear his laughing voice teasing her as he teased Mrs. Blestow, she longed to feel his lips on hers again. If she left she would never see him again, she would never hear his voice, never know what was happening to him, never know whether he was happily succeeding with his plans for Chickaroo, or whether he had set-backs and needed sympathy and encouragement, never know when he, too, fell in love with someone. She was aware suddenly that she was turning the knife into her own wound, but her thoughts gave her no peace. Perhaps he already was in love? No — she would not leave. She would stay — at least until Clinton returned.

At least she would do what she could to help, and she would see a little more of Lance, even if it hurt; and then she would leave. Perhaps she would go back to Geoff. Her pride felt a little comforted and as she remembered his love for her. Or perhaps she would stay on in Australia. She would have money enough to do that.

Her vague plans were brought to an abrupt halt by the entrance of Mrs. Blestow.

'I've brought you a hot drink,' she

told Diana. 'Mr. Lance told me you banged your head. It'll be best if you drink this and try to rest today. I'll send a lubra up from time to time to see if there's anything you want.' Her voice was so much more kindly than it had ever been that Diana felt helpless tears fill her eyes and roll down her cheeks. Fumbling in vain for a handkerchief she brushed them away with the back of her hand.

'Th — thank you,' she managed to say as she struggled upright to take the proffered cup. The housekeeper stood silent till it was drained, and Diana lying down again. For a moment their eyes met and then Mrs. Blestow said softly, 'It would be best for you to leave, you know. Whatever happens, Mr. Lance will always resent you.'

8

Diana's fall had shaken her up more than she had at first realised, and she spent the day in bed alternately dozing and waking. Occasionally a soft-footed lubra peeped round the door, and at dinner time two came quietly in — one to put on the lights and the other carrying a tray. With them, surprisingly, came Lance. Aware of her tumbled curls and sleepy eyes the colour came to Diana's cheeks as she sat up in bed.

'How do you feel?' Lance asked curtly.

'I'm fine, thank you. I've slept a lot.'

'No headache?'

'None at all.'

'I expect you'll have a few bruises, but if you still feel all right tomorrow, I'll meet you in my office at ten.' Diana could think of nothing to say. 'Mrs.

Blestow sent you up some dinner,' he went on.

'Thank you.'

He stood in silence as the lubra placed the bed tray over Diana's knees, and she held it steady. As the lubra left the room, Diana stole a quick look at Lance's face. He was staring at her hand as he had done in the office after she had impulsively stretched it out to him and he had ignored it.

'That ring,' he said suddenly. Diana glanced down at the topaz ring she had found amongst her mother's belongings. She remembered the pendant Geoff had bought her to match it.

'Oh, that,' she said lightly. 'It's nothing special. It's not even valuable.' The effect of her words startled her. Lance's mouth took a bitter twist and he laughed shortly and mirthlessly.

'Of course,' he said, 'you judge everything by what it's worth in terms of money.'

Diana's eyes narrowed in dismay, but she had no chance to reply.

'Eat your dinner,' Lance commanded, 'and I'll see you in the office at ten. It shouldn't take you long to find out how much Chickaroo is worth.' Then he was gone and Diana was left to puzzle over his remarks.

Surprisingly she was hungry, and even more surprisingly, once she had finished her dinner she was again ready for sleep. Next morning she dressed with particular care and presented herself at the door of Lance's office on the stroke of ten. After a brief, cool greeting he led her to a smaller room furnished with a large, flat-topped desk and several filing cabinets. 'If you're an accountant,' he said, 'I think the best thing I can do is leave you to it. You'll manage better, I expect than if I try to explain.' Diana realised with a pang of disappointment that she had been looking forward to sitting close beside Lance as he explained the books to her.

'All right,' she responded, trying to keep her voice cool.

'There are two sets of books,' Lance

told her. 'One for the running of the station, wages, expenses, incoming and outgoing — I'm sure you'll know all about that — The other set is investment records. Charles had a hard struggle to make the place a success, and when he began to succeed he decided that he wouldn't keep all his eggs in one basket. Half the profits were put back into the station, and half invested. No doubt you'll be relieved to know that even if the station loses money you will still have a decent inheritance.'

Diana made no reply. She must learn not to be so hurt by his unkind remarks, she thought, and she sat at the big desk trying to dismiss Lance from her mind.

She soon became so absorbed that she did not notice the passage of time. The books contained for her much more than mere figures, as she deliberately began by looking over the books of previous years; it was like reading a story. She read with amazement how much had been obtained for the sheep and how the money had been spent. The station hands she saw, had regular wage increases, and money was put aside for improvements to buildings and equipment. She missed lunch altogether, and by the time she realised that both her eyes and back were aching, she had a very fair idea of all that went into the books. She had found a clip full of receipts and another of bills, and she felt that on the following day she could plunge confidently into work. At dinner, she asked Lance. 'What do I do about bills?'

'Write a cheque and bring it to me to sign, together with the bill and an addressed envelope. Then they'll have to wait until someone is going in.'

'I — I haven't done much actual work today,' she confessed shyly. 'I've been reading back to make sure I get everything right.'

Lance did not even look at her.

'I'm sure it must have made interesting reading,' he remarked, and began talking to Tim. Determined as she was not to let Lance's remarks hurt her, Diana immediately began to talk to Johnnie. He seemed depressed, and thinking that he might be feeling homesick, she exerted herself to draw him into conversation.

When the meal was over, Lance did not, as usual, disappear, but followed Mrs. Blestow into the drawing room, fumbling in his pocket for his pipe as he went. Johnnie also hung back and murmured urgently to Diana, 'Come outside and walk a little with me. It's bright moonlight.'

The girl glanced towards the other room where Lance was settling into a chair opposite his housekeeper. She could not hear what he was saying, but he was smiling, that crooked, endearing smile which he seemed to have for everyone but her. She resented every moment that she could spend in his company and didn't, but perhaps if she were not there, he would miss her! Heady thought!

'All right.' She smiled at Johnnie, and

they walked out through the big front door together.

'One of the mares foaled yesterday,' Johnnie said. 'Shall we walk across to the stables and look at it?'

'If its mother won't mind being disturbed.'

'I shouldn't think so. Most mothers as far as I can see are just dying to show off their babies!'

Diana laughed.

'Come on then,' she urged. 'Let's go to the maternity ward.'

Together they strolled across past the drawing room window, and with all the will-power she could command, Diana refrained from looking in.

They stood together looking at the foal already independently standing, although perhaps with slightly wobbly legs.

'It's odd,' Diana commented idly, 'all babies are independent so very much sooner than human babies.'

They chatted desultorily about the mare and her foal, but Johnnie still seemed ill-at-ease. As he closed the door and Diana began to walk away, he clutched her arm. 'Are you quite all right now, Diana?' he asked. 'I felt so guilty when I heard of your fall; as if I hadn't taught you enough — or properly.'

'Nonsense!' she laughed, her voice a little shaky as she remembered the fall and Lance's arm around her, and his kiss. 'It was nothing to do with you, Johnnie, it was my own fault entirely, I was riding much too fast on hard ground.'

'All the same — ' his voice was subdued.

'Oh, come on, Johnnie,' Diana remonstrated, trying to rally him. 'No one is blaming you. Like I said, it was my own silly fault.' A thought came to her suddenly. 'Surely Lance hasn't blamed you!' she exclaimed.

'No,' Johnnie agreed. 'He hasn't mentioned it. The men have teased me a bit about it, though.' In spite of her sympathy for the boy, Diana felt a little impatient.

'You'll just have to get used to their teasing,' she murmured, beginning to walk towards the house again. 'I'm sure they don't mean anything malicious. You know that surely?'

Silently Johnnie fell into step beside her, and for a little way, neither spoke. Then Johnnie startled her by bursting out abruptly, 'They tease me because they can tell that I'm in love with you.'

'What?' Diana's voice carried all the astonishment she felt, and Johnnie's reaction was half-angry, half-pleading.

'Why does that astonish you?' he cried. 'I fell in love with you that first day we rode together — and Lance knew it, that's why he stopped the riding lessons so quickly. The men say I'm always gazing at you like a — well, they say I'm always looking at you, but what if I am? I never get a chance to see you alone; you never let me — '

'But, Johnnie,' she interrupted gently. 'You *are* seeing me alone tonight. I haven't deliberately avoided you, but — '

'Then you care, too?' he demanded eagerly, putting his hands on her shoulders and swinging her around to face him. 'Oh, Diana — '

She stood quite still. In the silver moonlight she could see his pleading eyes, and she hesitated a moment, wondering how to deal with this totally unexpected declaration of love.

Johnnie was probably her own age, but she had thought of him as just a boy; a pleasant enough companion, but certainly no more. Overwhelming awareness of her newly discovered feelings for Lance, however, made her realise how Johnnie might be feeling, and she sought for kindly words of dismissal.

With a tiny sigh she put her hands up to move his arms from her shoulders. 'Johnnie,' she began, but she was unable to go on. Completely misunderstanding, he flung his arms tightly around her and pressed his lips to hers. He was much stronger than she would have thought, and after the first stunned moment of seeming acquiescence, she struggled to release herself, but in vain.

'Johnnie, please!' she began as he lifted his head, but once again his kiss silenced her, and, angry now, she struggled even harder. Suddenly she was aware of someone quickly approaching, and she and Johnnie were dragged apart. An arm was around her shoulders, and she heard Tim's drawling voice say, 'Just happened by, and it seemed to me that you weren't all that happy at being kissed.' She saw his raised eyebrows in the moonlight. 'Just tell me I'm wrong and I'll apologise and be on my way.' He looked from Diana who was shivering a little, to Johnnie, who stood sullenly helpless in the grip of Tim's large strong hand.

'I — I — ' Diana stammered. 'It — it was a mistake. I — was — '

'As far as I'm concerned it wasn't a mistake.' said Johnnie fiercely, 'and I thought you — you — ' He stopped suddenly.

'I'm sorry, Johnnie. It was a misunderstanding.' She hesitated to say more in Tim's presence, but Johnnie gave her no option.

'You acted as if you loved me, too!' he declared. 'You let me think — '

'No, Johnnie,' she interrupted firmly. 'I didn't intentionally do that. I like you very much. I thought we were friends, but that's all.'

Tim shook him slightly.

'You hear that son?' he asked. 'That's clear enough. No misunderstanding possible there! So run along, and see that you don't bother Diana like this any more.'

'It's none of your business.' Johnnie's voice was low, and he stared at Diana for a second before flinging away.

'I'll get my own back on you,' he almost shouted at Tim, and then he ran stumbling back towards his own quarters.

Tim looked down at Diana.

'Puppy love,' he said indulgently. 'He'll get over it.'

'I — I never realised,' Diana admitted, 'and now — I'm afraid I've made him your enemy.'

Tim's laugh was not unkindly.

'It was my doing — not yours,' he said, 'but I don't think I would worry about young Johnnie. Come, I'll walk you back to the house.' He offered her his arm and they turned towards the house. As they did so, Diana became aware of Lance standing silently on the verandah watching them. How much of what had occurred had he seen? she wondered. Tim did not seem to notice Lance, and he chatted easily as they walked up to the front door.

'Thank you. Goodnight.' Diana took her arm from his.

'Sleep well,' Tim drawled, 'and don't let that little episode worry you. It'll all blow over, you'll see.'

Diana hesitated in the hall, glancing towards the drawing room. She did not want to miss the chance of any time spent in Lance's company, and he so seldom stayed after dinner, but she felt that she could not face the scrutiny of those piercing eyes or the possibility that he might remark on what he had seen. With a sigh she went along to her room. Poor Johnnie! I know what one sided love is like, she thought, but there is nothing I can do for him, except perhaps avoid him as much as possible. Perhaps she, too, should avoid Lance? But the thought was too bleak to bear. Every time she looked at him, or listened to him, she found something new to love — watching his hands as they dealt with his pipe, she imagined them caressing her; hearing his voice she imagined it deepening as he said, 'I love you, Diana.' Impossible dreams — but very sweet, and she could not give them up! Sooner or later she would have to leave, but she would hang on to the exquisite pain of being with him as long as she could.

Next morning she met Lance at breakfast, and was surprised and delighted when he said, 'I'm going to ride round the newer boundaries, and take a look at a few things this morning. Bring a note-book and come with me.'

The morning was sheer bliss, although as they rode off together she was aware of Johnnie's sultry eyes following them. Lance behaved as if he found her company pleasant, and he pointed out birds and flowers to her, and waited patiently while she wrote down things he had noticed which needed attention. They met one of the hands coming back from inspecting sheep further up the valley, and Diana sat dreamily in the sun with her back against a rock, while he and Lance smoked and discussed the animals' condition. All too soon they were riding back and were almost at the house when Lance's words shattered the pleasure she was feeling.

'I couldn't help seeing your romantic little interlude last night,' he remarked drily. 'I'd advise you to be careful how you encourage any of the men. Johnnie is obviously suffering from first love — but the others are experienced, grown men. Even so, I guess one or two of them wouldn't mind a chance of marrying half the station — whether they loved you or not!' For a stunned moment Diana stared at him speechlessly, reining-in her mount.

'You — you — ' angry words then tumbled out of her lips. 'I haven't encouraged anybody. But whom I encourage is no concern of yours anyway. I — I'll marry whomever I like — and — and — you should have more sympathy for Johnnie — can't you remember being in love?'

Lance pulled his horse round to face her.

'A rather muddled speech,' he commented, 'but no doubt you know what you mean. In case it needs an answer — yes — I can remember first love; but it usually passes, I do assure you, so don't go imagining you've blighted the boy's life. As for the rest — you will of course do exactly as you like. As for marrying — ' He paused.

'Well?' she demanded angrily. 'What

right have you to say anything about my marrying?'

'None at all,' he replied. 'You are utterly correct.' And he turned and rode on, leaving Diana with the cold feeling that that was not what he had really intended to say.

Wordlessly, side by side, they dealt with their mounts, and at lunch Lance talked animatedly to the others while Diana remained silent. Johnnie's place was empty, but no one remarked on it.

After a short rest in the afternoon, during which angry thoughts chased each other through her mind, Diana went down to Clinton's office. She would forget everything in bringing order to the figures. There was a rhythm and rightness about them which had often comforted her before. Today however, they failed miserably. She seemed all the time to see Lance's face and to hear his voice, and, after vainly trying to work for an hour, she put the books away and went for a walk.

She was a little late for dinner, and so

came into the middle of various comments about what had been heard in the 'chat session' over the two-way radio, an essential on every isolated sheep-station. Johnnie was there, but he did not look up at her. Diana wondered whether Tim — or perhaps Lance — had commanded him to be present. As she slipped into her place with a murmured apology, a few smiles greeted her, and the talk went on. She glanced round the table, listening with faint interest. None of the people mentioned were known to her, and she felt like an alien in the midst of all the chatter.

Charlie Wright had broken his leg. They'd have to rally round, Lance said, and he'd arrange something. Sharon had a new baby daughter. Bill must be pleased to get a daughter at last after four sons. The radio doctor was going on holiday, and there would be a replacement for a month. She knew none of these people, and supposed she never would. As she ate she enacted a happy little daydream in which she stayed at Chickaroo, and was soon as well known as all the people were. Perhaps she would meet other wives in Melbourne sometimes, to shop and to exchange more personal news. 'Other wives' — she blushed unnoticed at the trend of her thoughts, but doggedly clung to them. 'Diana's coming.' She imagined them saying. 'We'll have — ' but here her dreams were brought to an abrupt end. At first she wondered whether she had uttered her thoughts aloud! But no — 'Lisa's coming,' was what she had heard, and she looked around enquiringly.

'You were really deep in thought,' Tim's lazy voice said. 'Not listening at all to all the bits and pieces we're discussing.'

'I heard someone say 'Lisa's coming,' — but I never know the people you're talking about,' Diana said a little defensively.

Tim smiled.

'Well — you will get to know Lisa,' he stated. 'Lance is going in to fetch her tomorrow morning. Don't know how long she'll be here. Did she say?' He turned to look at Lance at the head of the table.

'No,' Lance replied. 'Just that she had a few free days and would like to come. Blessie,' he said, 'let me know if there's anything you want brought back, and,' looking round the table, he added; 'if anyone has any letters to be posted, I'd like them by seven tomorrow.'

After the meal the men dispersed, some, Diana guessed, to write hasty letters home. Lance went off to the kitchen with Mrs. Blestow, and Diana hesitated in the hall.

'No more trouble from young Johnnie!' Tim's voice half-asked, half-stated, as he stopped beside her. 'I told him he was to come in to meals and stop sulking. At the moment he wants to kill me, but he'll get over it.' At any other time these words would have disturbed Diana, but tonight her mind was on other things.

'Who is Lisa?' she asked.

'Lisa? Oh — Lisa Grange. She grew up on the station. She and Lance got acquainted with each other by radio long before they ever met or she ever came here; through the schools' programme,' he explained. 'She's younger than Lance but occasionally they had a talking get together for kids to discuss their hobbies — like stamp collecting and so on, and young Lance took a shine to her although he'd never seen her. I reckon she was *his* first love!' Tim chuckled. 'Anyway, later she came for a visit, and she's been coming ever since.'

Diana's heart felt like lead as she listened to him, but his final words made her feel a misery the like of which she had never known before. 'She's always welcome,' Tim went on. 'Of course out here where there is so little female company, *any* woman is, but Lisa turned out to be someone special. In fact, we all thought there'd be wedding bells before Clinton went away. Still — I guess it won't be long now.'

Diana bade him goodnight, and went numbly to her room. 'Lisa and Lance.' Her footsteps seemed to echo her thoughts. Now, for the first time she felt that she *wanted* to leave. How could she bear to see Lance with another woman? Tomorrow he would be setting off to fetch her, no doubt he would be up early, and thrilled at the prospect.

She would stay in her room until he had gone, she decided. But as she sat looking out at the waning moon and big stars, her pride stepped in. No, she wouldn't avoid him. She would be up at seven and she would give him a letter for Geoff. Putting on the light she took out her writing case, and began to write. Carefully keeping anything of her thoughts and feelings out of the letter, Diana wrote on and on describing her flight, her impressions of Melbourne and what she had so far seen and learnt at Chickaroo. She wrote nothing at all of Lance, lest the mention of his name, even on paper should bring all her feelings bubbling painfully to the surface again. At the end she surprised herself by writing:

'When everything is settled, I think I shall stay on in Melbourne, or perhaps visit some other cities. I might even try to get a job and stay on in Australia.'

It's not fair to write and let him hope that there's some future for us when I go back, she explained it to herself; but really she knew that however vain was her love, she didn't want to leave the country where Lance was.

9

Diana handed her letter to Lance next morning as he stood by the sideboard drinking a cup of coffee. He glanced idly at the address. 'Boy friend in England?' he asked lightly, but Diana pretended not to hear him and took her coffee and toast to the table.

'No breakfast, Lance?' Tim asked as he came in with several letters in his hand.

'I'll breakfast in Melbourne,' Lance replied.

With Lisa! Diana added in her mind, with a swift stab of jealousy.

'I'll be back during the afternoon,' Lance went on, 'but we ought to fix up pretty soon about sending some help over to Charlie's missus. Can I leave it to you, to arrange it, and to take someone over there?'

'Of course,' Tim answered. 'Actually,

it might be a good idea if I took young Johnnie. Several other stations around will be offering help and they won't need too many men just to make up for Charlie. Johnnie would be available for all the odd jobs, and that should be a help.' He hesitated, then went on. 'He's sulking around the place, and being as insolent as he dares. Just now he's not doing himself nor Chickaroo much good.' Diana, sitting with her back to the two men, ate her toast in rigid silence as a wave of red rose in her face. She felt tense and defensive as if they were about to blame her for Johnnie's behaviour; but Lance merely said, 'Good idea. Give my regards to Charlie and his missus.'

'Will do.'

'Doesn't seem as if any more letters are coming,' Lance went on, 'so I'm off. 'Bye.' His farewell was directed to no one in particular, and Diana ignored it, wishing with all her heart that he was not so happily going off to fetch his girl. She talked a little with Tim, and watched in awed fascination as he ate two big chops with tomatoes and chips.

'Is — is Johnnie being very difficult?' she asked hesitantly. Tim, with his mouth full, waved his fork in denial.

'No — not really,' he said when he could talk. 'He's reverted to behaving like a misunderstood adolescent — time he'd grown out of that, really; but I suppose, just living with a mother and sister, they've tended to spoil him.'

'I — I really didn't encourage him, you know,' Diana said.

'I'm sure you didn't.' Tim's voice was positive, 'but young Johnnie hasn't been used to being denied anything, I think. He's a good-looking lad, and I should imagine, could attract the girls. He's probably had quite a bit of success, but now for the first time, *he's* really attracted, and he probably just can't believe that you're not. In his heart I think he believes that I am the only one who stands between you.'

'Oh dear! What shall I do?' Diana asked. 'He seems so much younger than

I am, but he thinks of himself as a grown man.'

Tim chuckled.

'Oh, we all do that when we first begin to feel our feet,' he told her. 'As for age, I should think he's about the same age as you are, or not more than a year younger. Girls seem to mature so much more quickly,' he added reflectively.

'It's difficult to keep on avoiding him,' Diana said, 'and maybe I shouldn't do that anyhow?'

'That's why I thought it would be a good idea to send him away for a week or two,' Tim agreed. 'The more you avoid him, the more he'll try to get you alone. Perhaps a change of scene will turn his thoughts in another direction. I don't want to sound unflattering, but you know, Diana, sometimes first love dies as quickly as it blooms.'

'You're very understanding,' she smiled at him.

'I can remember my own first love,' he chuckled, 'but it's not really sympathy. At times in the last few days, I've felt very impatient with him. It's really that I want to keep the peace in the station.'

Diana was silent for a minute.

'My coming here hasn't exactly helped, has it?' she said at last.

'Oh, don't worry about that.' Tim, she noticed, did not deny her assumption.

'Well,' she said briskly, to cover the forlorn feeling which swept over her, 'I'd better go and get on with the books. At least I can be a bit of use in that way before I go.'

'When did you think of going?' The question held no special emphasis, but Diana saw that he was waiting for her answer.

'Oh, as soon as Clinton gets back, I guess,' she said, 'I'll go on keeping the books till then.' Tim received this in silence, and Diana, taking a deep breath, said. 'Nobody wants me here, do they?' Tim's level grey eyes looked into her brown, half-aggressive, half-pleading ones.

'There's not much room for women on a sheep station,' he said at last, 'except the housekeeper and the lubras, and perhaps the boss's wife; and — well — you can understand Lance's attitude. Most of the men feel the same way, I guess, even apart from their loyalty to Lance.'

'Clinton was friendly,' Diana cried, 'and he thought it would be a good idea for me to come.'

'Did he now?' Tim's voice was thoughtful. 'Did he maybe suggest it?'

'No. Why should he? But when I suggested it he didn't try to stop me.'

'No.' Tim's voice was still thoughtful. 'But you know there's not much love lost between him and Lance. In fact, I'm surprised that he hasn't left for another job before now. Still, I suppose good jobs with as many perks are hard to get. He should have understood and respected Lance's feelings though.'

'But it's not my fault!' Diana began passionately. 'My father — ' A blank look came into Tim's eyes, and she realised that it was useless to continue. Abandoning her pretence of eating, she got up and left the room.

In Clinton's little office she sat for a while, breathing heavily as if she had been running, and staring into space. At last, with a sigh, she stood up and began to collect the books she intended to work with.

Four hours later she sat again staring into space, but this time with something different in her mind. Perhaps she was being stupid and inaccurate because of the way she was feeling? But no — it couldn't be that! There was something definitely wrong with the books! Very wrong — too wrong for it to be just the result of her agitated emotions! The sound of the gong made her realise that lunch was imminent, and she went quickly to her room to freshen up before joining the others in the dining room. Neither Johnnie nor Tim were present.

'They're over at Charlie Wright's place,' Mrs. Blestow said in answer to her query. 'Didn't you hear the helicopter go? I expect Tim will be back later this afternoon.'

Diana was disappointed; she had wanted to question Tim a bit more about Clinton's not-so-good relationship with Lance. But perhaps it's just as well, she thought. I *must* be mistaken. I'll go over everything again very carefully this afternoon. But later, when she rose wearily from behind Clinton's desk, Diana was still of the same opinion. Something was very wrong. The next thing, she thought, was to find all the bills and receipts and correspondence for the last year. She had already heard Tim return, and soon the little plane would drone in with Lisa and Lance. She must make absolutely sure that she was right before she voiced her suspicions to him.

She pushed her fingers through her damp, unruly curls. She had been sitting for several hours tensely going over and over the figures before her, and now she felt that she could not face any more. I'll start early tomorrow morning, she planned, and go all through the papers as well as the books before I say anything to Lance. 'Lance!' Just thinking of his name made her realise anew how much he meant to her. How *can* I love him? she wondered, when he dislikes me so much — and obviously can't wait to get rid of me? Pictures of Lance drifted through her mind. No matter what happened or where she went, she would not be able to forget him. She could pick his voice out from among a thousand; and she knew that when she left she would always be looking out for a glimpse of that tall, spare figure. No — she couldn't leave Australia! Even though the knowledge of him married to Lisa would be torture to her, she knew that she would accept any crumb, any reminder, any sight or sound of Lance! Thinking of Lisa made her glance quickly at her watch. Soon they would be here. She would go and rest a little before they met at dinner.

In her room she took off her dress and lay on the bed, but although her body was resting, her mind went round and round in the same old circles. When she tried to stop thinking of Lance and Lisa, figures crowded into her head, and at last she gave up the attempt to nap, and decided to have a leisurely bath in the hopes that that would refresh her. As she ran the water she heard the little plane circling ready to land, and a hand seemed to squeeze her heart.

She took an inordinate amount of time over getting ready for dinner. She brushed her dark curls vigorously, and paid minute attention to her finger nails. For a long time she hesitated over make-up, but remembering how badly she had applied it before her first meal at Chickaroo, she decided on the merest touch of lipstick only. Looking at herself in the mirror, she half angrily pulled off the black silk dress that she had put on. She had bought it long ago, thinking that it would make her look more sophisticated and grown up. It hadn't done so then, and it didn't now. It just made her look too dressed up. She stood in front of the open wardrobe door and surveyed her clothes. Nothing seemed right. For a fugitive moment her sense of humour came to the surface. What dress would be just right for meeting the man you love and the girl he is going to marry, she wondered? At last she decided on a simple yellow sheath dress. It suited her well and showed off her slim figure to perfection; but Diana was in no self-admiring mood, and merely murmured, 'That'll do.' She took out the topaz pendant that Geoff had given her — so long ago it seemed — and slipped on a pair of high-heeled dark brown sandals. She was only just ready as the gong sounded, and with heart-beats which she felt could be heard all over the house, she walked to the drawing room. Everyone else, it seemed, was already there. Drinks in hand, they stood together chatting happily around Lance and his companion. With slight surprise she noticed that Johnnie was there, too. As on the first night it was Tim who came across to her, as she hesitated in the doorway, feeling that she wanted to run away.

'The usual?' he asked her with his lop-sided smile. 'Come and meet Lisa and then I'll get you your drink.' She followed him across to the little group which seemed to her to part reluctantly to let her in.

'It's real nice to have two women on the station for a while,' Tim said with an attempt at gallantry. 'Diana won't have to entertain us all on her own — ' His voice trailed away as if even he realised what nonsense he was talking. No one wanted Diana on the station! Tim had as good as told her so himself and certainly none of them were entertained by her! She looked sharply at him, but the evident chagrin on his face showed that he had spoken without thinking, and certainly had no malicious intent. She turned her head again and looked at the girl who stood before her. She had to look up a little, for Lisa was tall. Almost as tall as Lance. Diana's glance flickered to him for a second. What a handsome pair they made, standing side by side! In her mind she redressed them both in bridal clothes, and again a giant hand seemed to squeeze her heart.

Lisa was as fair as Diana was dark. A shimmering curtain of thick, blonde hair fell to her shoulders, and her eyes were as blue as Lance's. She had applied her make-up well, and she looked every bit of a sophisticated city girl. For a moment after Tim's disastrous speech, no one spoke. Then Diana's chin went up. No one was going to feel sorry for her! She'd see to that! She took a step forward and extended her hand.

'I suppose we don't really need introducing,' she said. 'At any rate it seems as if no one is going to do it. How do you do?'

The girl took her hand. 'Hi, Diana!' she said carelessly. 'How're you liking life in the Outback?' Without waiting for an answer she turned to one of the men.

'Another gin, please, sweetie,' she said. Tim was now at Diana's shoulder with her drink, and she was glad to have something to hold. As Lisa had handed over her glass, she had noticed a gleaming sapphire on the third finger, and she felt that she wanted to tear it off, to rip the black dress which Lisa wore so effectively, and to scratch the make-up from that perfect face. The intensity of her feelings frightened her, and as conversation became general she turned away and found herself face to face with Johnnie. 'Hello!' she greeted him with an effort. 'I didn't expect to see you here tonight.'

The sulky young eyes looked at her.

'I would have eaten with the hands,' he said, 'but Tim made me come in.' He immediately regretted having admitted that anyone could make him do anything, and hastened into further speech. 'I thought you might not want to see me,' he said, 'but Tim said you'd probably feel more embarrassed if I didn't come.'

'Oh, Johnnie. Of course I don't not want to see you,' she said impulsively, and then smiled. 'That sounds rather a muddle, doesn't it? What I mean is, please don't avoid me. Surely we can still be friends — even if — even if — ?'

'Even if you don't want me,' he finished for her in a low voice. 'You think I'm just a child. They all do. Even Charlie's wife didn't want me. She thanked Tim, and said she had enough volunteers to carry on till Charlie was O.K. again. Just as well. I *wasn't* a volunteer.' Diana looked at him in dismay. He was evidently still suffering a sense of grievance, and feeling snubbed by everybody.

'What's it like? Charlie's station?' She asked, hoping to encourage him to talk about other things and forget his introspection.

'I don't know. I wasn't there long.'

Sighing inwardly Diana persisted. 'But you had a meal there. You must have noticed the house.'

'Oh, it's all right.' He looked at her over the rim of his glass, and seemed to make some small effort. 'It's not as — as elegant as here,' he said, 'and the food's not as good.' Before she could encourage him even further away from his bad mood, the others began to drift towards the dining room, and they had perforce to follow. At the table, when as usual she had little chance to talk, Diana studied Lisa and Lance, turning the knife in her own wound. She could not keep her eyes from the ring on the girl's left hand, and at one point she became painfully aware of Lance looking from the sapphire on Lisa's hand, to her own topaz ring, and she remembered his scornful voice saying. 'Of course you judge everything by what it's worth in terms of money.' She bent her eyes to her plate and let the conversation swirl around her, only exchanging an occasional banal remark with one or other of the men.

'Engaged at last, then?' Joe said cheerfully. 'We were all beginning to think you two would never get around to it.'

Diana saw the quick exchange of

glances between Lisa and Lance, and saw that his brown hand momentarily closed over hers before he answered for her.

'There's a time for everything, Joe,' he said cheerfully. 'And it seems that the right time has come. Hasn't it, Lisa?'

'Too true!' she answered, with an odd inflection in her voice. 'The time is just perfect.' Diana looked puzzled. There seemed to be some hidden message in her words, and from the smile on his face, Lance had evidently read it correctly. Lovers secrets! Diana thought miserably, and the food in her mouth seemed suddenly hard to swallow.

'When's the wedding going to be? We're all looking forward to a jamboree!' Tim said, and Lisa laughed. A laugh, Diana realised angrily, that was as attractive as the rest of her.

'Well, obviously it can't be just yet,' she replied, 'but we both want it to be as soon as possible.'

Like a drowning man clutching at a straw Diana felt relieved that the wedding was not imminent, but she wondered why the reason should be so obvious to them all. Perhaps, she thought, they want to wait till they've got rid of me, and the inheritance has been dealt with.

Thinking of this, made her remember the worrying figures which she had totally forgotten in the last hour. No doubt Lance would be fully occupied with Lisa tomorrow, but she would shut herself away in the office and work again at those figures until she was utterly sure that she was right. Oblivious now to the rise and fall of the chatter around her, she decided that she would go and work after dinner. It was bad enough to be with Lance and his so-attractive fiancée during the meal. It would be even worse when there were fewer of the others around after dinner in the drawing room, and if they were not there she would torture herself imagining them in each other's arms in some quiet corner. She pushed her plate a little away from her, wishing she could leave at once. Almost she stood up, but, reluctant to draw attention to herself, she looked around and forced herself to listen to what was being talked about. Johnnie was glum and silent, but Lisa seemed to be engaging all the others in conversation.

'Actually I've given up my job now,' she was telling them. 'You won't know it, I'm sure, but it takes ages to amass a trousseau that is just right. I'll start when I go back to Melbourne; but what I really came here first for, was to help out with the books while Clint is away.'

'But you don't know anything about book-keeping, do you, Lisa?' Lance's voice was mildly surprised. 'I thought you only did secretarial work.'

'Oh, there's not much difference,' Lisa declared airily, and, as Diana knew, wrongly. 'And I've been to evening classes in book-keeping for some time. I'll take over till Clint comes back. It shouldn't be that long.'

'That's very sweet of you, Lisa,' Lance's voice was appreciative, 'but there's no need. You can enjoy your little break on the station before you start collecting clothes.' At Lisa's puzzled frown, he explained. 'Diana is an accountant, luckily for us, and she has taken over the books and will have everything straightened out in no time.' Was there just a hint of sarcasm, in his voice or did he mean exactly what he said? 'I guess she's started already, haven't you, Diana?' he went on. Diana hesitated; she was not yet ready to tell him what she thought she had discovered.

'Barely,' she answered, somehow producing a smile. 'I spent today looking over a lot of old books. I haven't really started on the current ones.' His eyes held hers for a steely second.

'Valuing the place — eh?' he said quietly, before he turned away to listen to Lisa.

'Well, if you haven't really started, I'll relieve you of the job.' She spoke across Lance, flashing a smile at the other girl. 'After all, you want to enjoy your break here, too, and I can come any old time.'

Diana's hands under the table were shaking with fury as she looked at Lance. Once again his eyes met hers, the expression in them enigmatic, before he turned back to Lisa.

'I think we'll leave things as they are, Lisa,' he said lightly, but there was no mistaking the determination in his voice. 'The station itself can't interest Diana that much, and the books evidently do. I'm sure she'd prefer to be occupied while she's here, wouldn't you, Diana?'

'Infinitely,' she answered with as steady a voice as she could manage; and Lisa shrugged her shoulders lightly.

'O.K. sweetie!' she said, 'but I feel quite hurt at having my offer of help turned down.'

'Rubbish!' Lance laughed at her. 'You can help us all by being as decorative as you always are.'

10

As soon as they left the table Diana excused herself and slipped away. She doubted whether anyone even noticed her going. Once again she stood in Clinton's office, where she seemed already to have spent so many puzzled hours. She went at once to the filing cabinet where she already knew that all receipts, bills and business letters were kept. It took her only a little while to realise that there was nothing there more recent than about ten months ago. Thinking that perhaps she had muddled the papers when she had looked through earlier years' accounts, she went through them all again, steadily and carefully. She did not find any recent papers at all. Perhaps Clinton was working with them until he left, and did not put them back in the proper place, she thought, reluctant to believe that he had steadily and systematically cheated his employer out of thousands of pounds.

She thought about Clinton as she sat for a moment before resuming her search. He had seemed to resent Lance, she remembered, had called him patronising, and he had helped her to come to Australia, almost glorying in the fact that Lance would be in some way discomforted by her presence! But if her reading of the accounts was correct, Clinton had begun to embezzle money long before Lance became the owner — the half-owner, she reminded herself — of Chickaroo. Surely he didn't dislike my father, too? she thought. He's worked here for several years, and presumably been treated as well as all the other men.

She cast her mind back, trying to remember all that Clinton had said. She remembered his saying Lance was 'just a nipper when I went there first. Later he went to the city to school, and to college. When he came back he wanted to take over, or at least take over a large part. I don't know what college had taught him about running a sheep station.' If she had thought about it at all, Diana would have imagined that perhaps he didn't like his boss being someone he had known as a mere boy; but that still didn't explain why he had been stealing, as Diana was by now dismally sure that he had been. She remembered the odd note in his voice when he had agreed with her surmise that he wouldn't mind Lance's anger about his helping and encouraging her to go to the station. What was it he had said? 'By then he'll have more things to blame me for than your unexpected arrival.' He had been almost gloating, she thought. Was he so sure of himself? He knew that auditors were going to be called in before the estate was divided. Perhaps he was counting on the fact that Lance would await his return so as to have all the books entirely up to date? Perhaps he intended never to come back? Impatiently she got to her feet.

Perhaps I'm also letting my imagination run away with me, she thought.

Quickly and methodically she began to search, but an hour later when she had handled every paper in the office, she had to accept the fact that the papers which mattered were missing! Suddenly she felt overwhelmingly tired. She seemed to have been in this little office for ever, and mostly with unpleasant thoughts for company. I'll put it all out of my mind, she determined, and start again tomorrow.

That, however she discovered, was easier decided than done. She tried to read in bed, but figures seemed to dance between her and the printed page. At last she gave up, switched off the light, and tried to compose herself for sleep, but sleep would not come. In vain she tried to find a comfortable position, and turned her pillow to find a cool place. The figures were successfully put out of her mind, but Lance and Lisa filled it.

After some hours spent vainly trying to woo sleep, she sat up and switched on the bedside light. It was just after one, she noticed. Quietly she crept out on to the verandah and sat in a cane chair, absorbing the warm air, the night noises and the scent of the flowers all round the house. The moon was even smaller now, and a silver crescent hung amongst huge stars. The sky looked like dark blue velvet. A night for lovers, she thought — but then angrily chided herself. What did she know about lovers? What did she know about love? Except that it took over and filled one's whole life; and was painful! She thought briefly of Geoff. It was so painful for him, too; and for Johnnie. She was not alone. Yet for some lucky people how wonderful it must be! To love, and be loved in return. Her heart ached as she thought of Lance and Lisa. She remembered the glances they had exchanged, and she re-membered the strong brown hand momentarily closing over Lisa's. How jealous she had felt then! How jealous she felt now! Life was unfair. Why, oh, why did she have to fall in love with the one man who only wished to be free of her presence? If only he had welcomed her to the station. If only he had told her all the many details she was longing to know about her father. If only he could have fallen as deeply in love with her as she knew she was with him!

Her hands clenched on the arms of the cane chair. This kind of thinking was foolish. Every moment that she stayed on would only add to her pain. She must leave, she thought, as she had already thought several times before, but she could not leave until she had finished her self-imposed job, however unpleasant its outcome. Once again her mind turned to the problem of the missing papers. Where could they be? Perhaps Clinton had taken them with him — never intending to return. Perhaps though — and she clung to this hope — the papers were somewhere available, and all the oddities would somehow be explained, and she was making a terrible mistake. But where could they be? Suddenly an idea struck her. They might be in his bedroom! That would seem a logical place! He might — as she had so often done, have taken them with him to take one more look over them before going to bed. Tomorrow she would look there. Hard on the heels of this thought followed another one. Why wait until tomorrow? She knew which was Clinton's room. Everyone was surely in bed by now? Sleep seemed far away. She would go quietly and search at once.

Quickly she put on a dressing-gown and slowly and very quietly opened her bedroom door. The house was long, low and rambling. It had evidently been added to as necessity and — or — money made it a good thing to do. She stood still for a moment, and was aware only of darkness and silence. Stealthily she walked along, one hand on the wall, not wanting to switch on any passage lights. At the door of Clinton's room she hesitated. There seemed to be the tiniest thread of light showing under the door! Her heart beats quickened, but in a moment she calmed herself. It's the moonlight, she thought, and swiftly and silently she opened the door and felt for the light switch.

It was unnecessary. All the lights in the room were on, and across it her startled eyes looked into Lisa's! For a second there was complete silence and they stood as if turned to stone, staring at each other. Lisa was the first to recover. 'Good heavens! You startled me, sweetie!' she said in a low voice. 'What on earth are you doing creeping into Clint's room in the middle of the night?' Diana pulled her dressing gown closer around her, inconsequentially but dismally aware of its sober practicality, as compared with the garment of blue silk and lacy ruffles which the other girl wore. She took a shivering breath. 'I might ask you the same thing,' she replied in as level a voice as she could manage. Lisa's delicately arched eyebrows rose and she laughed softly. 'Lucky Clint isn't here!' she smiled.

'Two women creeping into his room at night could cause quite a stir!'

'But he isn't here, and we are.' Diana felt calmer now, but this time Lisa's smile was not so pleasant.

'I can't imagine why I should be answerable to you,' she said slightingly, 'but if you want to know, I couldn't sleep, and I came in to look for some sleeping pills which I know Clint has.'

Diana was silent.

'Your turn now!' Lisa mocked.

'I thought I heard a noise,' Diana lied, 'so I came in to investigate.'

'How very brave of you, sweetie; well now you've investigated and found only me, so you can go back to catch up on your beauty sleep.'

'I'll help you look for the pills,' Diana said quietly.

Lisa held out a closed fist.

'I've found them, thanks,' she said shortly. 'I was just going when I heard you at the door. Unlike you, *I* was scared to death!'

Diana hesitated for a moment, but

there seemed nothing to do but go. 'Goodnight then,' she said. 'I hope the pills help.' She walked down the passage to her own room feeling frustrated and slightly puzzled. Clint hadn't seemed like the kind of person who would need sleeping pills — nor did Lisa; and in any case it was only just after one o'clock, surely a little early to decide that sleeping pills were so necessary that they warranted creeping into someone's room to look for them? She had not been aware of Lisa's following her from the room, and inside her own door in the darkness she looked back along the passage. The lights were still on in Clinton's room, but even as she looked, Lisa came out, switching off the lights as she did so. After a few seconds Diana closed her door and got back into bed. She lay puzzling over the events of the last few minutes. Had Lisa really been looking for sleeping pills? It seemed odd but Diana could think of no other reason for the girl to creep into Clinton's room when everyone else was in bed. There was another elusive fact which puzzled her, and she went over and over that brief encounter, trying to pick out what it was. At last she gave up and tried to put Lisa out of her mind, and at that precise moment, it came to her! She remembered her last glance of Lisa as she came out and switched off the light. She had been carrying her big leather hand-bag slung over her shoulder!

Alert again now, Diana thought over this new fact. Why on earth had Lisa taken her hand-bag with her to look for sleeping pills? It had not been in evidence as they confronted each other over the bed, yet in her mind's eye she could clearly see it looking incongruous and out of place against the blue silk and the lacy ruffles. What did it mean? Did it mean anything? She grew more and more puzzled. One thing was certain, however, she could not go back to Clinton's room tonight. Her search would have to wait until the morning, preferably when Lance and Lisa were out of the house.

Her chance came soon after nine o'clock. With mixed feelings she watched Lance and Lisa ride away side by side. Sternly she dragged her thoughts away from their jealous wandering, and hurried to Clinton's room. It was much the same as her room, only the curtains and covers were different. With no personal belongings lying about, the room looked bare and clean as if waiting for its occupant. Standing with her back to the door she glanced around. If Clinton had left the papers behind by accident they wouldn't still be here. The room had obviously been cleaned since he had left, and whoever cleaned it would have handed them over to the housekeeper, who would surely have given them to Lance or put them in Clinton's office. The only other alternative seemed that he had deliberately hidden them in order to postpone discovery; but why hide them? Why not destroy them? It might be difficult though to destroy them unobtrusively. There were no fires where they could be burnt. Still she would search, she thought, and crossed to the dressing table and began to pull open the drawers one after another.

In less than half an hour she was forced to realise that there were no papers to be found. The drawers were all empty, and the wardrobe very nearly so. She had felt in the pockets and linings of the few clothes still hanging in it and had climbed precariously on a chair in order to look into the little cupboard above the built in wardrobe — and found it empty; and she had even — panting a little — stripped the bed and turned the mattress. Nothing at all! As she made the bed with hands shaking with haste, she thought miserably of how and when she would tell Lance. They would be back for lunch — unless they had gone off for the whole day. She should not delay.

Back in Clinton's office she looked again at the books, and then suddenly slammed one shut and left the room.

She had been over and over those figures, nothing was going to alter it now! Disconsolately, she wandered out of the house. She would go for a ride, she thought, but almost immediately discarded that idea. She might come across Lance and Lisa, and even to see them together in the distance would be to invite fresh pain. Instead she decided to walk across to the stables and see the new foal.

There she found Tim who greeted her with a smile. 'It's a beaut, isn't it?' he said. 'Getting stronger and more independent every day.'

Diana stretched out a tentative hand, and the foal nosed at it inquisitively while his mother turned a protective head to see what was happening. For a while they talked idly about the foal, and Diana tormented herself by imagining that it was Lance who leaned with her over the low rail, and that presently he would turn and kiss her.

'I saw Lance and Lisa riding off,' she surprised herself by saying.

'Yes. They've just gone for a gallop,' Tim told her. 'They'll be back for lunch.'

'She's very beautiful.'

Tim shrugged his shoulders. 'I guess so,' he said.

'Don't you think she is?' Diana persisted.

'Yes — yes, I'm sure she is.' Tim sounded slightly uncomfortable.

'I suppose you must have known her for a long time?' Why was she going on talking about Lisa? she wondered. But the subject of Lance and Lisa was obsessive, and she could not stop herself.

'Well — yes. Ever since I came here,' Tim replied. 'She's changed a lot since she grew up and went to Melbourne. Become a real city sheila.'

'I wonder if she'll find it difficult to settle down on a sheep-station again.'

'I should think she'll find it impossible,' Tim said drily. 'In fact, I shouldn't think she has any intention of trying. They'll be living in the city in no time.'

Diana stared at him.

'Living in Melbourne?' she queried, in astonishment.

'Not necessarily Melbourne,' Tim said, 'but certainly not here. I'm sure Lisa's not about to give up city life.' Something in his voice made Diana look at him more closely. For all his surface friendliness last night it would seem that he didn't like this beautiful blonde girl whom Lance was going to marry. She hesitated over her next question.

'Surely Lance couldn't run a sheep-station from the city?' she asked him.

Now it was Tim's turn to look astonished.

'Of course not. Why should he? In any case Lance loves this place. I don't think anything would make him leave it.'

'But — but — ' Diana felt totally confused.

'Anyway there's no question of that,' Tim said with finality, as he straightened up and moved to the stable door.

'But, Tim — ' Diana moved beside

him. 'Surely you can't mean that after the wedding Lance will stay here and Lisa live in the city; and you just said that — '

'Hey! Hey! Wait a minute,' Tim interrupted. 'What's Lance got to do with it?'

Diana stared at him as if he had gone mad.

'When Lance and Lisa get married,' she began slowly, and Tim deepened the impression by throwing back his head and laughing. Diana could only stare at him.

'Listen,' he said at last. 'Lisa is engaged to Clinton. What made you think she was going to marry Lance?'

'Engaged to Clinton?' Diana could do nothing but echo his words.

'Sure. Oh, she and Lance had a thing going about a year ago. I don't think it lasted long though, and certainly there was never any talk of marriage. Then, about ten months ago things looked as if they were getting serious between her and Clinton.' Diana's emotions battled with each other for supremacy. Surprise, delight, and a hopeless feeling of 'what difference does it make anyway?'

'So she's engaged to Clinton,' she said slowly.

Tim nodded.

'We've all wondered if it would come to that,' he said, 'and now it has.' He paused, then went on. 'Actually it'll be a good thing if Clinton gets a job in the city. He's a very jealous type, and although Lance and Lisa were always very discreet, he may have guessed that they were more than just neighbourly friends. Or,' he added thoughtfully, 'she may have told him. She likes excitement, and it might have amused her to tell him.' Diana made no reply, and Tim said suddenly. 'But of course I shouldn't be talking about them like this. You won't repeat it, will you?'

'I'll forget you ever told me!' she replied, 'but I'm glad you did, or I might have made a fool of myself — and embarrassed them — by saying the wrong thing.'

Tim looked relieved.

'Yes. Yes, I suppose so,' he agreed. Diana's mind was in a whirl, and as they emerged into the bright sunlight she stumbled. Tim's arm saved her from falling, and for a moment she leaned against him, as he murmured, 'All right? Or did you twist your ankle?' Before she could reply a shadow fell in front of them and a furious young voice said.

'No *wonder* you warned me off Diana! You had your eye on her yourself! Creeping off together to the stables when no one's around. And you — ' he almost shouted, glaring into Diana's astonished face.

He got no further. Tim's arm was removed from Diana's shoulder, his fist shot out, and Johnnie was suddenly flat on his back, one hand to his jaw. For a second he lay stunned, and then he scrambled to his feet and rushed at Tim, fists clenched and lips drawn back in a snarl. Tim reached out his long arms and put a hand on each of Johnnie's shoulders, effectively holding him off.

The boy's flailing fists scraped Tim's ribs, but seemed to occasion him no pain at all.

'Stop it, you young fool!' Tim said firmly, but Johnnie was beside himself with rage, and kicked out at the other man's shins. Tim shook his head slightly and then, releasing Johnnie's shoulders, he slapped his face so hard that the boy fell to the ground again.

'Oh, please!' Diana cried.

'Don't worry. There's not going to be a fight,' Tim assured her. 'I don't fight with children.' He leaned over the boy. 'Enough is enough,' he said sternly. 'Diana doesn't want your attentions, and whatever she does is no business of yours. Now pull yourself together and grow up! You're no use to yourself or anyone else while you behave like this! I'm not sure it wouldn't be a good idea for Lance to get you transferred to some other station.'

Johnnie raised himself on one elbow in the dust. His face was discoloured and there were tears in his eyes.

'I'll be glad to go!' he half-shouted, half-sobbed, 'but I'll get my own back on you before I go! Just you wait and see.' Without answering, Tim took Diana's arm and led her towards the house. There were tears in her eyes, too.

'Oh, dear. It's all my fault,' she said. 'I should have stayed in England.'

'Nonsense!' Tim shook her arm lightly. 'I had to hit him, Diana; heaven knows where this nonsense would have ended otherwise. I'm sorry for the boy. First love is a painful thing, especially if it's not returned, but he has to grow up. He can't go through life expecting no disappointments or set-backs at all. The best thing now will be to behave as if none of this happened. To the young, loss of dignity is almost as bad as loss of love.'

Tim left her at the house and she went slowly to her own room where she sat on the side of the bed trembling slightly. How right Tim was! First love, especially if unrequited — was a very painful thing. I'd better grow up, too, she told herself; but as she sat and thought over all that Tim had told her, she found it hard to be out of sympathy with Johnnie. Even when the dream seemed unobtainable it was hard to let it go. Lance and Lisa, Lisa and Clinton. The names went round in her mind. Again she saw Lance's hand close over Lisa's, and she realised now that it had just been a gesture of affection. All else between them was finished, and he was glad that she was going to marry Clinton.

11

Once again Johnnie was missing from the table, and Lance commented on his absence. 'He's O.K.,' Tim said briefly. 'We had a difference of opinion, and he's probably sulking.' Lance's eyes swept speculatively over Diana, leaving her in no doubt that he had seen Johnnie kiss her on the moonlit night.

'The boy's too old to sulk,' he said. 'We'll have to knock him into shape or he's never going to be any good.'

Tim smiled wryly at Diana.

'I'm doing my best,' He told Lance. 'I'll just go on as if nothing has happened; he'll grow out of it.'

'He's here to work and to learn,' Lance said coldly. 'Not to be nursed through growing pains. If he doesn't soon pull himself together he'd better go!'

'Oh, no!' Diana said impulsively, and

Lance's eyes searched hers.

'Do you have some special reason for wanting him to stay?' he asked in a smooth cool voice.

Diana subsided.

'No. No, of course not,' she murmured, aware of Lisa's bright eyes laughing across the table at her discomfiture. She looked steadily back, and was satisfied to see Lisa's eyes drop before she began to talk to Lance.

Diana hardly noticed what she was eating. She put Johnnie and his troubles firmly out of her mind, and began to think of Lisa and Clinton. If he had been embezzling money, did she know about it? Thoughtfully she ate and pondered about what would be the best thing to do. She suddenly heard the word 'bank' and jerked her attention back to the table.

'They seem to want to see me about something urgent,' Lance was saying. 'You could go in and find out what it's all about, Tim; and if they do really need me. I don't want to leave right now. Go in this afternoon, have a night on the town, and come back tomorrow.' Did Diana imagine it, or did Lisa give her the briefest possible glance before she said gaily, 'I could do that chore for you. Now that I live in the city I don't get nearly enough chances to fly a chopper or a plane. I'll be glad to do it.'

Lance smiled at her.

'You're only just here, and you want to leave again!' he teased. 'I don't think you'll ever really be able to settle down to station life.'

'Maybe not.' Lisa's smile was brittle, 'but I was only wanting to help, and I miss flying myself.'

'Oh, you can fly the chopper when I take you back,' Lance promised carelessly, 'but don't rush off now. Tim can go.' The subject was closed, but Diana felt a little thrill of excitement. If Lisa had gone, would she have come back? Her swift offer to go — completely uncharacteristic, Diana guessed — seemed to indicate that she had guessed Diana's suspicions and wanted to leave as soon as possible.

She would tell Lance about the books at once, she decided, as soon as she could get him alone. Almost she opened her mouth to say that she would like to speak to him alone after lunch, but second thoughts made her pause. She would ask him when Lisa was not there. Lisa, however, lingered on, and finally Tim and Lance excused themselves, leaving Mrs. Blestow and the two girls at the table. Mrs. Blestow began to question Lisa about the latest cinema shows in Melbourne, and Diana took advantage of this to slip out after the two men. She had no chance to get Lance alone, however, for she found him just outside with Tim, and Johnnie. Johnnie's voice was raised in anger, but she did not catch what he said. By contrast Lance's voice was icy.

'Don't tell me we've got to release you, boy! From what I hear of your behaviour lately, there's no way we would want to keep you. Get on with whatever you're supposed to be doing now, and I'll deal with you later.' He strode away.

'Fuel up the Cessna for me, Johnnie,' Tim lingered long enough to say. 'I'll be going into Melbourne later.'

An angry retort seemed imminent, but after a furious glance in Diana's direction, Johnnie turned on his heel and strode away in much the same manner as his employer had done. Tim shrugged and smiled ruefully before he followed Lance.

Obviously now was not the time to get Lance alone, and Diana went slowly into the house again. In the hall she met Lisa, who merely smiled briefly and went to her room. Diana wandered restlessly about, hoping that Lance would soon return to the house. At last she could stand the inaction no longer, and she rashly decided that she would go and talk to the other girl. Perhaps Lisa would let slip something to confirm Diana's suspicions.

There was no question of 'letting slip'. Lisa opened the door to her and smiled sarcastically when Diana's eyes opened wide at the sight of her packed suitcase standing by the door.

'Well, well! If it isn't the great detective!' she exclaimed. 'Come in, and don't look so surprised. Surely you didn't expect me to stay here, did you? after you've made it so obvious that you've discovered what's been happening?'

'You — you knew all the time?'

'Of course I did, sweetie! It was my idea; and we would have been long gone before anything was discovered if we hadn't had such bad luck. First the old man died and you had to be found, so that meant auditing the books much sooner than it would normally have been done. We got over that nicely by Clint asking to be the one who came to see you — saying that he also wanted to trace his father.'

'He said he didn't want anything to do with his father.' Diana was momentarily side-tracked.

'Of course he didn't,' Lisa said

scornfully, 'but Lance believed him. And then you came out — which wouldn't have mattered to us at all if you hadn't turned out to be an accountant, of all things!'

'But — but *why*?' Diana cried. 'Why should you want to do this to Lance, and why should Clinton?'

'There's never been any love lost between Lance and Clinton,' Lisa said. 'It was just one of those things. Clint envied Lance his father, his money — everything; and particularly he envied the fact that Lance and I had something going.'

'I still don't understand. If you — if you loved Lance — '

'Who said anything about love?' The answer was vehement. 'We just suited each other. We'd known each other for years, but when Lance came out of college he was suddenly grown up. We had an affair, and it should have ended in marriage. If he'd left me for someone else it wouldn't have been so bad, but just to get tired, to say 'we'd grown out

218

of each other'! Nobody can do that to me.' Her voice was hard and the blue eyes had narrowed into venomous slits. 'So,' she went on, 'I determined to have my revenge. It took a little while to figure out that the best thing would be to hurt Chickaroo.'

'But my father — '

'Oh, I know — Charles was still alive when I talked Clint into it, but I knew that everything would be Lance's eventually, and whatever the station lost would be his loss, too.' She laughed shortly. 'And you sweetie, have helped just by your very existence — because everything that Lance has got now, he has to share with you! Clint was a fool,' she went on. 'His neat little accountant's mind wouldn't let him destroy papers. He was quite sure they would be safely hidden for a long time in his room. Then he discovered that you were an accountant, and he phoned me in a panic. He had already sent a message pretending to have had an accident, and he was suddenly afraid that you might offer to do the books which of course you did! Obviously you were interested in finding out what the place is worth. Well — now you've found out! It's worth quite a bit less than it was!'

'You came to try to keep me away from the accounts!'

'Of course!'

'Why are you telling me all this?' Diana cried. 'You won't get away with it, you know!'

Lisa's smile was like the touch of an icy finger.

'Oh, yes, I will!' she triumphed. 'I know that Lance is riding out to the four mile boundary this afternoon. By the time he gets back, I'll be long gone. I've already given up my flat, and it'll be easy enough to lose myself in Melbourne till I join Clint.'

Diana stared at her, remembering her offer to fly in to the bank for Lance.

'You can fly,' she remembered audibly.

'That's right, and there's nobody here right now to stop me.'

Diana remembered with sickening dismay that the other girl was right. Everyone would be away just now except Mrs. Blestow, and she would be no help even if Diana could persuade her in time, which she very much doubted! Perhaps Johnnie was still around? Or would he be avoiding everybody? Suddenly she whirled and ran from the room, followed by Lisa's mocking laughter. She would get Lance, she thought wildly — that seemed the only thing to do. Perhaps he would not believe her, or be in time either, but she must tell him, she should have done so before.

With trembling fingers she saddled the mare, jerking the girths tight with unusual impatience. Soon she was mounted and wheeling round in the direction of the four mile boundary. She only hoped that Lisa had been right and that that was where she would find Lance. From the corner of her eye she saw Johnnie standing near the big shed where the Cessna was kept, but she did not hesitate. Her mind was set on getting to Lance. She was wearing a summer dress, and her legs, without the protection of jeans, were rubbed and pinched on the stirrup leathers. Biting her lip she ignored the discomfort and urged the mare to an unwilling gallop. She had not gone more than a mile when she saw a horse coming towards her. Lance! It must be Lance. At almost the same moment the rider spotted her, and his mount's pace increased. Lance galloped up to her, his face concerned.

'What is it?' he demanded urgently. 'Has there been an accident?'

For a moment Diana hesitated, words tumbling over themselves in her mind. How could she explain everything quickly enough?

'It's Clinton — Lisa,' she said jerkily as their horses stood facing each other. 'He's — been cheating you out of lots of money; and Lisa's been helping him. It's true, Lance — please believe me.'

Lance stared at her.

'I've had my suspicions for some time

that he was doing some petty thieving,' he said, surprising her, 'but he'd been with my father some time — with Lisa — well, it was rather a delicate situation.' He sounded a little uncomfortable. 'Anyhow,' he went on hastily. 'I knew she'd want him to leave and live in the city once they were married, and that would end it all without — well — without a fuss.' Diana said nothing and he went on, 'But why have you come rushing to tell me this now?'

'Lance — Clinton has embezzled thousands of pounds, at Lisa's instigation,' she said urgently. 'She came to try to stop me finding out, and now she's packed and she's got the year's accounts, probably the books, too, and — ' she stopped, and they both looked and listened as the helicopter could be seen and heard rising ponderously into the air like some monstrous insect.

'She's taken the chopper!' Lance cried.

'That's what I came to tell you.'

He reached across and grabbed the mare's bridle, pulling her round parallel with his own mount.

'Hang on,' he said, 'you tend the horses when we get back, and I'll take the Cessna. I'll be waiting for her when she touches down in Melbourne.' Unashamedly Diana clutched the pommel of her saddle and gave up all efforts to ride properly as the horses galloped neck and neck back to the stables. Lance helped her to dismount, and while she stood breathing heavily, with trembling legs, and holding the two pairs of reins, he ran towards the little plane. Diana tethered his mount and led her own inside; when she came out to get Lance's, she heard the first sound of the plane's engine.

Johnnie suddenly appeared beside her, his face white. 'Lance,' he said. 'Lance is using the plane! I tried to tell him, but he just yelled 'Get out of my way!' Oh, God — Diana!'

'Tell him what?' Diana stared in surprise at the boy's shocked face.

'I — I drained most of the petrol *out* instead of putting more in,' he told her in panicky haste. 'I — I thought Tim was going to use the Cessna, and I wanted to pay him out for — for — I thought the plane wouldn't start, and he'd have to fill it himself; but perhaps it *will* start, and then crash — and Lance wouldn't listen — I — '

'You fool! You stupid little fool!' Diana's heart was in her mouth with fear for Lance, and almost before the words were out of her mouth she was on his horse, hanging on grimly as she kicked it into a gallop straight towards the plane, oblivious of danger. Pulling up, she half-slid half-fell to the ground, letting the horse go, and ran breathlessly to the plane. Lance stood in the tiny entrance.

'You little fool!' he was yelling, unconsciously echoing her own earlier words to Johnnie. 'You might have been killed!'

'Y — you, too!' Diana panted, as she half climbed, half scrambled up to him.

'The plane,' she gasped. 'No fuel. Johnnie — '

'I've got to go,' Lance said, 'if I'm to intercept Lisa I can't hang around. Go back now.' He put his hands out to turn her and help her down, but Diana sobbing now, and with strength born of desperation, pushed past him into the passenger seat.

'If you insist on going, I'm going, too,' she gasped. With a strange look on his face, Lance closed the little door.

'All right, we'll go together,' he said quietly. Trying to master her sobs, Diana was aware of the plane bumping slowly along, increasing speed, and then leaving the ground. For a minute there was silence as the ground fell away from them, and then Diana found her voice again.

'Lance!' she said, the words tumbling over each other in her urgency. 'You don't understand. There's hardly any fuel. Johnnie drained it off instead of filling it up. He — he had some stupid notion of inconveniencing Tim, but the plane will crash!'

'How do you know?'

'He was frightened. When he couldn't stop you he came to me.'

'The sooner he goes the better,' Lance commented. 'Of all the crazy, irresponsible things to do.'

'Yes. Yes. But Lance — what can you do?'

He turned his head and smiled briefly into her agonised eyes. 'Only one thing to do,' he replied briefly. 'If there's no fuel I'd better land as soon as I can.'

Diana clasped her hands tightly together in her lap.

'Will — will it be all right?' she shivered.

Lance did not answer. He was scanning the countryside ahead, and after a few tense seconds, he turned the nose of the little plane towards the ground. Diana let out her breath in a long sigh as they touched down and bumped along to a standstill.

'Oh, Lance!' She buried her head in

her hands and began to shiver uncontrollably.

'Out,' he said briefly. 'Come on. I'll help you. What with only that thin dress and the shock — you need to be in the sun.' Carefully he helped her to descend. Never had firm ground seemed so wonderful. Hastily he stripped off the sheepskin jacket he was wearing and put it round her shoulders, leaving his arm there to hold it in place. Still shivering she clung to him, and buried her head on his chest. 'Oh, Lance,' she sobbed, 'I thought you'd be killed. I couldn't bear it!'

'So when you couldn't stop me you decided to come with me and be killed, too!' he said, a strange new note in his voice. 'Diana, my darling! My brave, foolish darling!'

For a second her shivering stopped, and then started again as she lifted her head and looked incredulously into his eyes.

'Wh — what did you say?' Her teeth

were chattering, and her whole body shook. Lance led her across to a huge, sun-warmed boulder.

'Let's sit against this,' he suggested. 'I'll hold you close and make you warm, and then I'll say it again.'

Sitting together he held her tightly in his arms and murmured words of endearment until gradually her shaking stopped.

'Look at me, Diana,' he commanded; then, shyly and disbelievingly she raised her eyes to his.

'It was a lovely dream! You really didn't say — '

'I love you, Diana,' he interrupted, bending to kiss her upturned and tear-stained face. A little later he went on, 'I was prepared to hate you, but somehow you made me love you almost from the first moment I saw you; and my hard feelings withered away no matter how much I tried to keep them alive. Oh, darling — you will marry me, won't you? Please, Diana — please love me, too!'

'I do,' she whispered and lifted her face again for his kiss. When Lance spoke again he tightened his arms around her, and with a forefinger tilted her face so that he could look into her eyes.

'Lisa has no real reason to hate me. We drifted into an affair together. God knows I would have married her early on, but she said she didn't want to marry me. We'd just enjoy each other and then inevitably grow out of each other and find someone new. After a few months I found that she was right, but by then she'd decided that she *did* want to marry me. There seemed to be no hard feelings though, and I was relieved when so soon afterwards she seemed to be falling for Clinton.'

'She was using him to have her revenge on you,' Diana said. 'She told me so before she left. I couldn't stop her, and now — now you won't be able to either. You will probably have lost a lot of money, Lance.'

'*We* will,' he reminded her. 'Half of

everything is yours you know.'

'I don't care about the money, whether we lose it or not, as long as you are safe,' Diana said, passionately pressing closer to him. 'Oh, Lance — kiss me again.'

When next they were capable of coherent speech, Diana raised her soft brown eyes to his blue ones which were looking at her with love and faint puzzlement.

'What is it?' she asked.

'I fought against it so hard,' he said, 'but I couldn't stop myself loving you, even though I wanted to hate you because of the way you treated Charles. Why — oh, why did you treat your father so badly, Diana?'

She stared at him in blank astonishment.

'He accepted that when you were small your mother was right and it was better that he shouldn't visit you or take you out and perhaps upset you, but she agreed that as soon as you were old enough to understand, the choice should be yours. Charles kept a photo of you always on his desk, and he waited patiently until you were about nine or ten before he tried to contact you; but he thought of you often. From then onwards until he died his one ambition was to get to know you as his daughter. He wrote first to your mother and then to you — regular, hopeful letters. He sent birthday presents and Christmas presents every year. The letters were never answered and the presents never acknowledged. He asked for photographs and begged you to see him, either here or in England.

'I adored Charles, you know. Ever since he first married my mother, and even more after she died. From the time I was about seventeen I used to watch him gradually giving up hope as the weeks passed after every letter or present was posted to you. I hated you, and used feverishly to imagine myself taking all kinds of revenge on you. The last present he bought you I helped to choose. Your topaz ring. Topaz because it is your birthstone. He so hoped that would please you. With it he wrote yet another letter pleading with you and begging you to come at least for a holiday. The letter was returned, torn in half!' He paused. 'And when I met you the ring was on your finger, and you told me it wasn't even valuable! Why, Diana? I don't understand. It's not like the you I've grown to love — or am I forgetting Charles in my love and need for you?' There was a kind of anguish in his eyes, which turned to tenderness as he saw the tears rolling down her face.

'I didn't know, Lance; I didn't know.' She drew a shuddering breath. 'My mother told me my father had died when I was two. She would never talk about him. I — I didn't know about the presents — or letters — and I found the ring when I was sorting out my mother's belongings.' She looked down at the topaz ring which had so suddenly acquired a new meaning. 'I was so surprised when I heard that my father had only recently died,' she went on, gradually controlling her voice, 'and — and I came out here hoping to find out what he was like — but no one would talk to me about him.'

'My poor sweet . . . How badly we've used you!' Gently he touched the ring. 'Wear it always,' he said, 'and we'll go and buy an engagement ring for your other hand; but I warn you that I'm not prepared to wait out a long engagement.'

Diana blushed and put her hand in his.

'I — I'd like this to be my engagement ring,' she whispered. 'Does that seem silly to you?'

'It seems perfect,' he said as he carefully drew the ring from her right hand and slipped it on to her left, and then carried it to his lips.

'Even if Lisa and Clinton get away with it, we shan't be poor,' he promised her.

'I wouldn't care!' she told him passionately. 'As long as I have you!' For a little while again there was silence as they sat close together in the sun, each looking forward to a rosy, beckoning future. Lance stirred at last. 'Well, we'd better be getting back,' he said, and releasing her, he stood up and extended a hand to pull her up.

'Getting back? You mean *walk*?' She said as she stood beside him.

He smiled down at her.

'You look like a teddy-bear wrapped in that jacket,' he teased. 'No, my darling, not walking; we'll go in the Cessna.'

'But — but Lance — '

He interrupted her with a kiss.

'Johnnie will have my thanks though I'll never tell him so!' he said. 'If it hadn't been for him I wouldn't have realised that you love me, too, and you might have gone out of my life! But his childish attempt at revenge was more stupid than malicious. Every pilot checks fuel and instruments automatically before a flight. Even if he has just seen a plane refuelled — it's an automatic drill. I didn't know why

Johnnie hadn't done as he was told, but I knew he hadn't, and I planned to curse him for his slackness about obeying a order, and so making me lose time.'

Diana stared at him.

'*Why* didn't you *tell* me?' she demanded.

'I was so busy realising that you loved me, I suppose.'

'It doesn't matter now,' she murmured, slipping her hand into his. 'Time is all that was lost, and perhaps money — and we've gained so much!'

'Dear Charles,' Lance said, looking down at her. 'How pleased he would be to know that the very best legacy he left us both was each other!'

Other titles in the Linford Romance Library

SAVAGE PARADISE
Sheila Belshaw

For four years, Diana Hamilton had dreamed of returning to Luangwa Valley in Zambia. Now she was back — and, after a close encounter with a rhino — was receiving a lecture from a tall, khaki-clad man on the dangers of going into the bush alone!

PRETTY MAIDS ALL IN A ROW
Rose Meadows

The six beautiful daughters of George III of England dreamt of handsome princes coming to claim them, but the King always found some excuse to reject proposals of marriage. This is the story of what befell the Princesses as they began to seek lovers at their father's court, leaving behind rumours of secret marriages and illegitimate children.

A DREAM OF HER OWN
Barbara Best

A stranger gently kisses Sarah Danbury at her Betrothal Ball. Little does she realise that she is to meet this mysterious man again in very different circumstances.

HOSTAGE OF LOVE
Nara Lake

From the moment pretty Emma Tregear, the only child of a Van Diemen's Land magnate, met Philip Despard, she was desperately in love. Unfortunately, handsome Philip was a convict on parole.

THE GOLDEN GIRL
Paula Lindsay

Sarah had everything — wealth, social background, great beauty and magnetic charm. Her heart was ruled by love and compassion for the less fortunate in life. Yet, when one man's happiness was at stake, she failed him — and herself.

THE ROAD TO BENDOUR
Joyce Eaglestone

Mary Mackenzie had lived a sheltered life on the family farm in Scotland. When she took a job in the city she was soon in a romantic maze from which only she could find the way out.

THE VAUGHAN PRIDE
Margaret Miles

As the new owner of Southwood Manor, Laura Vaughan discovers that she's even more poverty stricken than before. She also finds that her neighbour, the handsome Marius Kerr, is a little too close for comfort.

HONEY-POT
Mira Stables

Lovely, well-born, well-dowered, Russet Ingram drew all men to her. Yet here she was, a prisoner of the one man immune to her graces accused of frivolously tampering with his young ward's romance!

MYSTERIOUS STRANGER
Brenda Castle

Jarrett Ross's arrival in King's Lacey, on the Norfolk coast, brought into question Adria Crayne's relationship with Tim Merrick, who loved her. Soon, Adria found herself falling in love with a man who might only be able to bring her pain.

FOR LOVE OF OLIVER
Diney Delancey

When Oliver Scott buys her family home, Carly retains the stable block from which she runs her riding school. But she soon discovers Oliver is not an easy neighbour to have. Then Carly is presented with a new challenge, one she must face for love of Oliver.

THE CAPTAIN'S LADY
Rachelle Edwards

1820: When Lianne Vernon becomes governess at Elswick Manor, she finds her young pupil is given to strange imaginings and that her employer, Captain Gideon Lang, is the most enigmatic man she has ever encountered. Soon Lianne begins to fear for her pupil's safety.

PAST BETRAYALS
Giulia Gray

As soon as Jon realized that Julia had fallen in love with him, he broke off their relationship and returned to work in the Middle East. When Jon's best friend, Danny, proposed a marriage of friendship, Julia accepted. Then Jon returned and Julia discovered her love for him remained unchanged.

NEW BEGINNINGS
Ann Jennings

On the plane to his new job in a hospital in Turkey, Felix asked Harriet to put their engagement on hold, as Philippe Krir, the Director of Bodrum hospital, refused to hire 'attached' people. But, without an engagement ring, what possible excuse did Harriet have for holding Philippe at bay?

THE SPANISH HOUSE
Nancy John

Lynn couldn't help falling in love with the arrogant Brett Sackville. But Brett refused to believe that she felt nothing for his half-brother, Rafael. Lynn knew that the cruel game Brett made her play to protect Rafael's heart could end only by breaking hers.